CHARMING THE BEAST

The WOLVES of WHARTON
Book Five

CHARMING THE
BEAST

BEAU LAKE

4 Horsemen
Publications, Inc.

TABLE OF CONTENTS

PROLOGUE (OTTO) VII

CHAPTER ONE (FLORA). 1

CHAPTER TWO (DOMINIC) 12

CHAPTER THREE (FLORA) 19

CHAPTER FOUR (DOMINIC) 26

CHAPTER FIVE (FLORA) 33

CHAPTER SIX (OTTO) 38

CHAPTER SEVEN (DOMINIC) 43

CHAPTER EIGHT (FLORA) 50

CHAPTER NINE (OTTO) 56

CHAPTER TEN (DOMINIC) .66

CHAPTER ELEVEN (FLORA) 75

CHAPTER TWELVE (OTTO) 80

CHAPTER THIRTEEN (DOMINIC) 88

CHAPTER FOURTEEN (FLORA) 95

CHAPTER FIFTEEN (OTTO) 102

CHAPTER SIXTEEN (DOMINIC) 109

CHAPTER SEVENTEEN (FLORA). 122

CHAPTER EIGHTEEN (OTTO) 135

CHAPTER NINETEEN (DOMINIC) 143

CHAPTER TWENTY (FLORA). 157

CHAPTER TWENTY-ONE (DOMINIC) 167

CHAPTER TWENTY-TWO (FLORA) 184
EPILOGUE (DOMINIC) 193
ACKNOWLEDGMENTS 199
ABOUT THE AUTHOR BEAU LAKE 201

PROLOGUE
(OTTO)

———◁◆▷———

My imagination—or rather, my current lack thereof—is a curse.

Just after midnight, I brew a cup of coffee, resigning myself to another sleepless night. I feel as though my latest film script has gained sentience; it argues with me, shaking off my words like droplets of rain. Every sentence I tap out on my Smith-Corona typewriter ends up balled up on the floor, kicked under the couch, or launched into the dark corners of my study. I don't dare throw them away; it would be like lobbing off the head of the Hydra. I imagine drowning under the weight of millions of paper balls, made heavy with half-sentences and diatribes.

I drink my coffee black, letting the bitterness settle on the back of my tongue. Then, I chase it with a drag from my menthol cigarette. The caffeine and nicotine in concert make my fingers tingle, and I flex them above the keys.

Write!

But I can't bring myself to make a single keystroke. The ink will only ruin the page—a blemish that, once made, I can't wipe away. I unravel one of the most recent castaways still on the desktop, reading:

It was a dark and stormy night. Daphne felt uneasy...

"Unimaginative dreck," I grumble. If I give MGM a prosaic, run-of-the-mill flick, I'll be finished. They expect excellence. I've delivered it before. I glare at the statuette sitting above my mantle, the crackling fire turning its slim, gold-plated body into a beacon. My name adorns the base: Otto J. Lang, Best Director, *Crazed (1946)*.

I should have been mediocre. It will hurt terribly to fall from this great height. I stub out my cigarette in my amber-colored ashtray, adding the filter to the pile.

I should take a walk.

Yes, that will help. Surely, it will shake the cobwebs loose. I just need a change of scenery. I've been staring at the blank page for far too long, under the disdainful eye of Oscar. I should take advantage of all of the tools at my disposal, shouldn't I?

Typically, when I tell industry cohorts that I live an hour outside of Los Angeles, I am met with wide eyes and wrinkled brows. They are all firmly rooted in the city, toiling away in vermin-infested apartments, just in case they get the opportunity to boast *I live just five minutes from Hollywood and Highlands*. But I prefer the solitude of the Santa Ana Mountains.

In L.A. proper, I felt small, trodden upon by hundreds of others vying for my position. But in Black

Star Canyon, it's just me, myself, and I. When I walk the dirt paths, packed firm by the hooves of cattle, I often don't see a single soul—especially at nighttime. The ranchers who work the rugged landscape go to bed before the sun goes down.

I walk for a mile uphill. It feels good to pant, to toil in a purely physical way. The trail becomes indistinct up here; the ranchers tend to stay down in the basin, where their animals won't twist an ankle or fall into a crevasse. Tall California buckwheat plants brush against my legs, and I can't help but think of rattlesnakes even though I know they are sleeping in their burrows.

Enormous limestone boulders mark the entrance to a long-abandoned silver mine, and I clamber up onto one of them to get an unobstructed view of the night sky. Some of the bored teenagers who live out here have carved graffiti into the soft rock. I trace a lopsided skull and crossbones, initials encased within a valentine heart, and a Killroy whose oblong nose has been altered into an elephant's trunk.

The stars above are numerous and impossibly bright; in the canyon, there is no pollution to obfuscate them. If I screw my eyes up just right, I can find Ursa Major, the great ladle in the sky. I imagine it stirring up the other constellations as though they are in a large pot, tangling Cassiopeia with Centaurus.

Suddenly, I hear a low growl in the distance. It must be the wind whipping down the mountain. I've lived out here long enough to hear the wind scream, the earth groan, and the sage scrub whisper.

"Hello?" I call, immediately feeling foolish. My voice echoes. *Hello-lo-o*. Of course, no one answers. I'm utterly alone.

But now, my solitude feels reckless. I can't help but think of the stories that persist about the canyon: murders, massacres, and mayhem. This land harbors ghosts. I'm not entirely sure whether I believe any of the tales of hauntings, but the growl sounded genuine enough.

I head home, keeping my eyes on the tiny light deep in the canyon's basin. It's the porchlight of my cabin — my north star. In my peripheral vision, the amorphous shadows seem to take shape, resembling the hulking grizzlies that once made this region their home. *There are no bears in the canyon*, I soothe myself. *Not anymore*. Still, I break into a jog and reach the established cattle trail in half the time.

My porchlight grows brighter. *Nearly there*.

I pass the sign for the Atkins' Ranch and consider making a beeline down their winding driveway. *But what would I possibly say?* I can't be sure I'm being followed. They'll just see me as a city slicker, out of his depth, balking at shadows like a horse too green to be under saddle.

Instead, I continue on my way, hurrying past fields of dozing long-horned cattle. *They would bolt if there was a predator nearby, wouldn't they?* I let out a shaky breath and, with it, a nervous laugh.

My cabin is just west of the Atkins' property and butts up against a small crater lake. When I hear the water lapping against the bank, I finally slow my pace.

But as soon as I step into the porchlight's warm glow, the light blinks out. Startled, I yelp.

Plunged into darkness, I dimly hear the tinkling of glass. "Hello?" I call, hesitantly inching forward. No one answers, of course; there's no one there. The bulb simply overheated; that's all. I climb the porch steps and fumble amidst the inky blackness for the doorknob. Glass crunches beneath the soles of my hiking shoes.

I'd left the door unlocked, as is the custom out here. "We're all friends in the sticks," Lionel Atkins had told me just after I bought the property, his ropy arms resting on the fence rail, "and we ain't thieves, besides."

Just as I open it, the growl sounds again. It's closer now, reverberating through my chest wall. With a strangled shout, I throw myself through the threshold, slamming the door shut behind me.

For a long moment, everything is still. I stand on the braided rug in the foyer, panting. Then, the doorknob jiggles. "Who's there?" I shout, sliding the deadbolt as the knob begins to slowly turn.

"I have a gun!" I add as an afterthought. It's a lie—I have nothing of the sort, just a Louisville slugger and a dull Bowie knife.

The doorknob stops, mid-turn. Then, laughter comes from the other side of the door. There are several voices: a boisterous guffaw, a tinkling titter, and a muffled snigger. It's an ostensibly human sound but makes me feel more on edge than the growl. Animals are dangerous. Humans, conversely, are cruel.

"Get off my property," I yell. I rush to my bedroom and pull the baseball bat from under the bed. Slowly,

I inch back toward the foyer, turning lights off as I go. If I can't see them, I don't want them to see me either.

It's not lost on me that I wrote a scene just like this in *Crazed*. In it, the female protagonist dances in the mirror, wearing only panties, her only companion a bottle of Prosecco. Throughout the scene, she is unaware that the killer is standing on the terrace, knife in hand. He can see every inch of her. But to her, he's just a shade among shadows.

In the living room, I turn off the green banker's lamp upon the desk. The rotary phone sits beside the typewriter, and I turn the dial to call the Atkins' residence. Lionel has a double-barreled shotgun mounted above his fireplace.

"Is it loaded?" I had asked him, curious.

"What good is it, otherwise?" He had laughed, taking it down to show me the Winchester brass inside. He let me hold it, and I was struck by how heavy it was.

The phone rings, and rings. No one picks up. "Shit!" I groan, dropping the receiver back onto the cradle. I consider calling the police, but they are miles away.

I can still faintly hear the chortling outside; it seems to come from every direction, as though they are surrounding the cabin. *How many are there?* I readjust my grip on the baseball bat's tape-wrapped handle, my palms slick with sweat. I haven't been in a fight since high school when Jake Crawford broke my nose and left me spitting teeth onto the sidewalk. Surely, I can't take on the intruders if they breach the locked door or break a window.

Something scrapes against the nearby bay window. At first, I think it was only the branch of the looming

Coastal Oak tree. Its thick, contorted trunk curves toward the awning, its branches draped across the rooftop like a lover's arms. I've been meaning to hire someone to cut it back before it damages the shingles.

But then, someone whispers, "I see you." It's a raspy voice, as though the speaker has swollen tonsils. It makes my skin crawl. I wrench the curtains across the glass, too frightened to search for the speaker in the velvety blackness.

Then, the howling starts. They are taunting me, pretending to be wolves. The person outside the window barks loudly before picking up the chorus.

My only feasible option is to hide. Clearly, these people are unhinged. I retreat to the bedroom and wedge myself into the cluttered wardrobe. Sandwiched between an ironing board and a gaggle of moth-infested winter coats, I try to calm my panting. I'm far too tall for the space, and I have to slouch, my chin against my sternum. The bat dangles from my right hand, the cool metal resting against my naked calf. In the dark, I quickly lose track of time. My muscles go stiff. Pins and needles coarse through my extremities. I wonder if this is what it feels like to be buried alive.

After a while, I realize that the howls and tapping have stopped. I squeeze my eyes shut, as though it will enhance my hearing. It's quiet. They must have moved on, bored of tormenting me. Mustering what remains of my courage, I ease open the door a sliver, a foot, and then the remainder of the way. No one jumps from the shadows to accost me, nor does the racket outside start up again.

I walk stiff legged through the cabin, bat at the ready, finding it quiet. In the living room, I inch back the curtain, peering out. My eyes have adjusted to the dark somewhat, and I can just make out the trunk of the oak tree and, beyond it, the still water of the lake. The yard is empty.

It was a bunch of dumb kids, I reassure myself. *Just kids sowing their wild oats. After all, what else is there to do out here?* I think of the graffiti I found, the content immature and silly.

Just some dumb kids.

I sink into the desk chair, resting my chin on my palm. As soon as I'm off my feet, fatigue courses though my body, gumming up my defenses. I should stay awake, I should—

—my chin clunks hard against the desktop, waking me. The sun is up, tendrils of diffused light leaking through the curtain's waffle knit. My neck spasms; my middle-aged body is not accustomed to sleeping at my desk. As a college-aged man, I would pop up, as refreshed as if I had slept on an innerspring mattress with the most crisp, cool sheets imaginable. Now, I'll be sore for days. I may as well have been hit by a car.

I long to crawl into my bed, but first, I need to be certain the interlopers are well and truly gone. Before unlocking the front door, I hesitate. *What if they're outside, waiting for me?* Whether it's bravery, stupidity or exhaustion, I unlock the door and swing it open. I inch through the threshold with the bat at the ready.

Outside, the air is chilly and as refreshing as a cool bath. *Crunch.* I look down to find glass from the ruined bulb beneath my feet. The shards seem to sparkle in the half-light of morning. I step off the patio, walking a few feet down the path.

Then, I find them: footprints in the dirt. They aren't mine from the night before. I was wearing boots, and when I kneel to get a better look, I see five individual toes. The owner of the print was barefoot—a dangerous, foolhardy thing to be in the land of rattlesnakes and cacti.

I look for more, walking around the side of the house. Near the oak tree, I find another and wish I hadn't looked at all. This one isn't a naked footprint, nor even a boot print. It is a canine's paw print, except ten times larger. Each of its nails left a deep divot in the soft ground, all longer than my index finger. *The howling!*

They weren't humans at all.

CHAPTER ONE
(FLORA)

———◁◆▷———

I've never been on an airplane before.

I gather the courage to ease open the window shade a few hours into the flight and immediately slam it shut again. The dizzying view of the halcyon sky, with its woolly clouds close enough to touch, makes me feel nauseous. I find myself staring at the emesis bag tucked into the seat in front of me. "For your convenience, from your friends at Delta!" is written upon the edge in a jaunty, strangely optimistic script.

I'm so accustomed to having my feet firmly planted on the ground that being airborne feels like an affront against my very nature. After all, my paws are molded by the terrain upon which I run, my muscles are primed to hunt ground-dwellers, and my keen nose can parse flora from fauna. Up here, all I can smell is stale, recycled air. I find myself rubbing incessantly at the gooseflesh prickling on my arms, fearful that my wolf's reddish fur will burst forth; she is frightened and wants to run. But there's nowhere to go.

1

Every minute in the air means miles between myself and the pack. It feels like pulling oneself away from magnetic north. Will our connection be broken somewhere over the Midwestern plains? Will it feel like being ripped apart? I groan, pressing the heels of my hands into my eyes. *This was a mistake.*

"First time?" the woman sitting beside me asks. Like all of the other passengers, she's dressed in her Sunday best, though she's sporting a velveteen sleep mask trimmed with black lace over her eyes. She pulls it up onto her brow, giving me a disdainful look. "You're *fidgeting.*"

"I'm terribly sorry. It's my first time," I reply.

"And you *had* to choose a cross-country flight?" The woman wrinkles her ski slope nose. Despite her advanced age—her face delineated by deep-set wrinkles—she sits bolt upright, her ankles primly crossed, her hands in her lap. While most of the other passengers are slouching or dozing, she looks as though she is posing for a photograph.

"I'm moving to Los Angeles," I say, gripping the armrests as the plane bucks, pummeled by an errant gust of wind. Or is it a sign of impending engine failure? Perhaps a hijacking, rerouting us toward Cuba.

It's strange to say the words aloud: *I'm moving to Los Angeles!* I had thought I would live in Wharton, Virginia until the Grim Reaper knocked upon my door, scythe in hand. Most Whartonites died in the same saltbox house they were born in. I fantasized about leaving, of course, but never spoke the words aloud. It was a lark, that's all. That was, until I met Carver Merlotte.

I can tell he's from the West Coast as soon as he walks into the office, Goyard branded suitcase in hand. There's something patently modernist about him; form follows function. Every movement is efficient, as though he mapped out the room before entering. Despite the heat and the less-than-reputable lodgings in which he's found himself, he is dressed in a tan, worsted wool suit jacket with high-waisted, pressed trousers.

As soon as he approaches the desk, he pulls a business card from his breast pocket and slides it across the countertop as though it's as valuable as a bundle of hundred dollar bills. "CARVER MERLOTTE, Talent Scout & Agent Extraordinaire" is printed upon the ivory cardstock in block letters.

Mr. Merlotte shifts from foot to foot as I neatly print his name in the leatherbound ledger. "How long will you be staying with us?" I ask, my pen poised.

"Just the weekend." He rests his weathered hands on the countertop, the knuckles thick and swollen. There's a ring on his finger, the discolored skin seeming to balloon around the gold band. It's too small, and he's clearly been wearing it for decades.

"Do you need two keys?" I ask. "For Mrs. Merlotte?"

"It's just me," he replies, fishing a crumpled pack of Lucky Strikes and a Zippo from his breast pocket. He lights it and takes a drag while I finish filling in the ledger. The smoke makes the air fuzzy until the oscillating fan sweeps it away. He idly examines the hand-painted travel posters tacked to the wall, most of which are for nearby Virginia landmarks: the historic towns of Jamestown and Williamsburg, the naval yard in

Norfolk, and the various beaches along the coastline. Most of the posters are outdated, the paper oxidizing and the edges curling away from the cinderblock wall.

When I hand him the key to room twelve, he makes no move to leave the cramped office. "Say, Flora," he begins, reading my name tag, "have you ever considered acting before?"

"Me?" A hot blush creeps up my neck.

"You have the face for it," he replies. "The cheek-bones of a Gene Tierney and the girl-next-door appeal of a Judy Garland."

"How flattering!" I chuckle. "Do you often use that line to chat up young women?"

"I'm a married man," he reminds me coolly, flashing the too-tight ring. "For twenty-five years—happily, in fact. I'm an agent and talent scout, as you can see on my card. You might know some of my clients. Have you ever heard of Chantelle Boucher?"

Chantelle Boucher's face is plastered on every Marshall Field storefront, advertising her latest fragrance: Fleuriste. This spring, she had a small part in the film Father of the Bride, *alongside Spencer Tracy, Joan Bennett, and Elizabeth Taylor.* Everyone *has heard of her. "I bought her perfume," I reply.*

"I'm in town to attend the Miss Dogwood Pageant," Mr. Merlotte explains. "I found Chantelle at a pageant in Lafayette, you know. She got third place; those backwoods goons didn't see what was so special about her. But I did." He puffs up his chest, proud.

"I'm competing in that pageant. I did some community theater as a kid. I played Peaseblossom in A Midsummer Night's Dream." *I don't tell him I fainted*

just after entering stage left, unable to deliver my first word of dialogue in act three. "Ready," I was meant to say, but only managed "re—" before swooning.

"Have you ever thought about moving away from here?"

I've always perceived California as a bastion of idealism: dreamy and lustrous, thickly populated by model-types and movie stars. Surely, it is the antithesis of my hometown, which can only be described as "sleepy." Or rather, "narcoleptic." Los Angeles, conversely, moves at top speed: luxury vehicles speeding down Route 101, heading toward auditions or premieres at Grauman's Chinese Theatre; pedestrians speed-walking, hoping to get a table at Ciro's or The Brown Derby; and fame itself, an amorphous, insatiable monster, chewing up bodies and spitting them out onto the sidewalk.

I imagine being in the laundromat and looking over to see Ingrid Bergman sorting her socks. Or Orson Welles at the malt counter. Would they become as familiar to me as my friends in Wharton? Oh, hello, Humphrey Bogart, how's the family?

Later that night, Ama Chilton adjusts the angle of my chin with the tips of her cool fingers, applying mauve lipstick to my plump lower lip with her free hand. Then, she carefully fills in my Cupid's bow, her brow furrowing in concentration. "How are you feeling?" my friend asks, retrieving a tissue from the box on the vanity.

Before I can answer, she places the tissue between my lips, so I can blot the excess product. I obediently close and open my mouth, leaving the perfect impression of my lips on the paper. "Nervous!"

"I don't think I've ever seen you nervous before a pageant. You look like you've swallowed a pill bug."

I feel like I have; hot, acidic bile edges up my esophagus, but I swallow it down. I reach for my purse and pull out a packet of antacids. Crunching the chalky, thick tablets between my teeth, I grimace. "It just feels so hinky, knowing someone is watching who could change your life."

Ama unscrews the top of the mascara and plunges the wand into and out of the inky black liquid. "Do you really think you'd go?" Her tone is curious, but there's a tinge of apprehension there too.

"Oh, I don't know. It's a good opportunity, isn't it?" I reply. Ama sweeps mascara onto my lashes, her upper lip quirked in concentration. "I can't say I've never dreamt of it. Hollywood, I mean. I just don't know if I have what it takes."

"If anyone belongs there, it's you," Ama relents.

A woman in a chiffon gown peeks into the communal dressing room, holding up three well-manicured fingers. Her nails are the color of clotting blood. Curtain call is in three minutes, and all of the contestants must be onstage for the opening number. We're singing a rendition of The Andrews Sisters' I Can Dream, Can't I?

Ama pops out of her folding chair as if spring-loaded, grabs the can of Liquinet, and douses my pinned curls one last time. Once satisfied with her handiwork, she places her hands on my bony shoulders, leaning down to kiss the top of my head. She meets my

*eyes in the mirror. "Good luck, Flora," she murmurs
before hurrying out to find her seat in the audience.*

*When the contestants are called to the backstage
area, I take my place in the chorus line. Through a
gap in the heavy curtain, I catch a brief glimpse of
the audience before the house lights go down. It is not
difficult to find the rotund talent scout; he's sitting in
the front row, his elbows infringing on his seatmates'
armrests. A leatherbound notebook sits upon his lap,
and he twirls a pen between his arthritic knuckles.*

*The first harmonic notes of the Andrew Sisters'
song begin as the lights dim, and I take a deep breath.
When I burst from the curtain, stage right, I sing my
line in a clear soprano.*

*Carver Merlotte's self-satisfied smile is as lumi-
nescent as a beacon.*

The woman laughs, interrupting my reverie. "Los
Angeles? A little slip of a girl like you? Honey, that
town will chew you up and spit you out."

"What makes you say that?" I ask, the now-familiar
churning of my stomach reaching a fever pitch. It's
as though someone is stirring my innards with a large
wooden spoon, sloshing bile up my esophagus. It's been
happening regularly since I signed with Mr. Merlotte's
agency, a symptom of uncertainty and anxiety.

"You have stars in your eyes," the woman remarks.
"Just like I did. But they'll all blink out in time, and
you won't be able to find your way."

"Are you an actress?" I ask. There's something
familiar about her, though I can't place her. It's
something about her hair—tight grey ringlets with

thin coppery strands interlaced throughout. A vague memory washes up, but it is too water-trodden to decipher: a woman's crooked smile, red curls bouncing, and the intertitle on-screen: *What fun!*

"I was, years ago," she answers.

A stewardess approaches our section, pushing a drink cart, and my seatmate raises her hand. "Could I get a sidecar, dear? One for my foolish friend too."

I open my mouth to protest, but the older woman shushes me. "I was in fifty-odd pictures, playing bit parts. I married a man who was Hollywood royalty, which made me royalty too. But it all inevitably comes to an end, doesn't it? He cheated on me, and our divorce ruined my career. Not *his*, of course."

The stewardess hands me a cocktail glass, the fluorescent yellow liquid inside sloshing. I take a hesitant sip, mostly out of politeness; I don't want my seatmate to think I'm ungrateful. "I'm really sorry to hear that," I reply.

"It's all in the past, darling," the woman says, patting my hand. She takes a glug of her own drink, downing nearly half. I wonder if she's telling the truth. "But if I were you? I would take the next plane home," she adds, swiping a bit of dampness off her bee-stung lips.

♦ ♦ ♦

I am met in the terminal by a short woman holding a bit of card stock with my name printed upon it. Her hair is a shocking platinum blond, piled atop her head in a loose chignon. It washes out her face, making her look ill.

"Flora Wright?" she asks, when I approach, lugging my overstuffed carry-on bag. "I'm Ingrid Parsons, your publicist." She has to raise her voice to be heard above the din. The terminal is crowded, and all around us travelers reunite with their families or run to find the gate for their connecting flight.

"I have a publicist?"

"You have one temporarily," Ingrid replies. "Carver Merlotte hired me to babysit you." *To babysit me?* The thought of having a babysitter feels somewhat demoralizing. But I also feel rudderless. Having someone's hand to hold is a relief.

The woman from the plane catches my eye as she passes. A young, harried man carries her bags, having to trot to keep up with her long, elegant strides. "Good luck, Flora," she calls before disappearing into the deluge of bodies.

Ingrid's green eyes bulge. "You know Bernadette Von Fleischer?" she hisses.

"Yes ... well, I mean ... no. She sat beside me on the plane. Who is she?" I stand on tiptoes, trying to catch one final glimpse of the woman. But I can't find her amongst the sea of fedoras and bouffants.

"She's only the most infamous actress of the 1920s. She hasn't worked in ages because she was blacklisted." Ingrid takes my bag from me. "Come on, kid. We've got to get on the road before the Harbor Freeway becomes a parking lot. You're staying at the Hollywood Roosevelt."

I don't put up a fight when Ingrid calls me "kid." While she appears no older than I am, she traverses the bustling airport and parking lot with the confidence of a seasoned pro. I follow in her wake, looking around with wide eyes. It's brighter in California, and the asphalt beneath my heels bakes. Even the air feels different, lacking the humidity that makes Wharton feel like sunbathing beneath a wet blanket.

In Ingrid's car, I stare out the window as we merge onto the freeway—a concrete behemoth with eight lanes. It's mid-construction, fluorescent orange vehicles and crews loitering on the shoulder, seemingly doing nothing at all. "First time?" Ingrid asks, giving me a sidelong look. She's smoking a cigarette, the window cracked. The meager breeze ruffles the whorl of hair resting upon her brow.

"I've never been anywhere but Virginia," I answer, my nose against the windowpane. "Where are all of the trees?" From the highway, all I can see is a concrete metropolis: squat warehouses, soaring high-rises, and cookie-cutter neighborhoods of identical, ranch-style homes.

Ingrid shrugs. "What you see is what you get." She points at a scraggy little palm tree, boxed in by two incomplete concrete pylons. "Unless you're living up in the canyons. There are plenty of trees if you're rich enough."

Hollywood Boulevard is teeming with people crossing in front of cars without a moment's hesitation. I catch a brief glimpse of Grauman's Chinese Theatre, its forecourt reminiscent of a Chinese palace, pedestrians staring at the hand and footprints of celebrities outside. But Ingrid doesn't linger, beeping the horn. She only deigns to slow when we approach our destination. The hotel is a twelve-story rectangular building, the words "HOTEL ROOSEVELT" adorning its roof like a tiara.

Ingrid leads me inside, and without stopping at the front desk, climbs the Spanish-style staircase. "You're up on the second floor. Tomorrow, you have breakfast scheduled with Carver down in the ballroom. Then, at noon, cattle call," Ingrid says over her shoulder, trotting up the stairs two at a time. I move more slowly, dragging my bag.

"What's a cattle call?" I pant. On the second floor, Ingrid leads me to room 229, unlocking the door.

"Carver must like you," she says, ignoring my question. I'm not entirely sure whether it's because she didn't hear me or because she found it beneath her. "This is the largest suite in the place."

It is a massive room, larger than four of the Cove Motel's guest rooms put together. All of the furniture inside—a sofa, a king-sized bed, and an Eames-style armchair—is stark white, and the table, meant to seat four, is made of glass. I am afraid to touch anything for fear of ruining it. "This is amazing."

Ingrid remains in the doorway. "The script for tomorrow is on the table. Carver will be in the ballroom at nine o'clock sharp. Don't be late. He hates when people are late."

"The script for—?" I begin to ask, but Ingrid is gone.

CHAPTER TWO
(DOMINIC)

"You have a meeting in an hour," Ramón says, rapping his knuckles against the doorframe. As soon as I open my eyes, the midday sun lances directly into them. With a groan, I pull the cool, goose down comforter over my head.

Someone left the curtains open.

"Cancel it," I croak. I take his silence as acquiescence. But when I tentatively peek out, Ramón is still there, arms crossed over his barrel chest. The sun makes his auburn hair fiery, tendrils of flame licking against his pressed collar. He's still wearing his clothes from the night before, though they are considerably more rumpled than I remember.

Ramón grasps the bedsheets in his fists and wrenches them off me. The naked woman sharing my bed squeals, running to the en-suite bathroom and slamming the door behind her. I clap my hands over my own nakedness. "Ramy!"

"Up and at 'em," he says coolly, unaffected by his childhood nickname. It usually makes him as pliable as underworked dough. This meeting must be important. I wish I could recall who it was with.

I grumble but swing my legs over the side of the mattress. "My head hurts," I pout, hoping he will give me some sympathy. Just one measly morsel.

"There are six empty bottles of Veuve Clicquot on the living room table." Ramy strides into my walk-in closet and pulls clothes indiscriminately off the hangers. He's not being careful; the wire *pings* as it stretches, leaving the hangers misshapen.

"I didn't drink those by myself." I remind him.

"I had two glasses," he replies.

Ramón dumps an armful of clothes into my lap: a roll-neck Cardin sweater, pressed, brown slacks, and a pair of briefs. The sweater will be far too hot in the California sunshine, but I pull it on without complaint. I know better than to whine; I can see the vein pulsing against his temple.

"The ladies had a few drinks too," I counter, but I've already lost the will to argue about it. I *did* drink too much. The hangover is akin to agony: a throbbing behind my eyes and an acidic mire where my stomach once was.

Ramón taps his toe while I dress, glancing at the crystalline face of his Rolex. When I am fully clothed, he tosses a pair of loafers into my lap. "Come on, we're going to be late. You know Jack Felton hates to be left waiting." Bending down to slip on my shoes makes hot bile course up my esophagus, and I have to swallow it down.

13

I follow Ramón into the living room. "Jack from MGM?" I ask, stepping over a brunette woman asleep on the floor, her cheek resting on her bare forearm. She's wearing one of my white undershirts and nothing else. I vaguely remember kissing her the night before, then kissing her friend.

A flaxen-haired woman lounges on the overstuffed couch, drinking a glass of flat champagne, presumably pilfered from the bottles left on the console table overnight. She props her heels on the armrests, her delicate feet encased in sheer stockings, toenails painted red. A pair of heels rest upon her lap. "Remember," she says, "you're trying *not* to lose your contract, Dominic."

"Who let you in?" Much to Ramón's dismay, I pause, my attention diverted. Penelope and I broke up months ago—the entire sordid tale available for all to read in *Confidential*. "This isn't your house anymore. You can't just come in whenever you'd like, Penny."

"Ramón did," she replies sweetly. "And you're lucky I stopped by. He was still dozing when I knocked."

Ramón grabs my arm, giving me a sharp tug toward the front door. "We have to go."

Penelope rolls her eyes. "Relax, Dom. I was just coming to get a few of my things. I left my furs in the attic."

"It's ninety degrees outside," I huff. "Surely, you could have called. I would have dropped them off later."

"I also knew you had a meeting this morning and that you would undoubtedly sabotage yourself somehow. I did you a favor." Penelope slips on her heels and rises to give me a chaste, dry kiss on the corner of my mouth. "Try not to say anything stupid to Jack Felton. I'll make sure your *guests* get home safe, and I'll lock up before I go." She smells earthy and sweet, like the milkweed one can find all over the valley.

It's a scent that makes me think of running down Brush Canyon after nightfall, the lights of the city upon my left flank. Penelope, in her lithe, wolfish form, was always the first to reach the Hollywood sign, her gums pulled away from her incisors in a triumphant grin. Often, she would lift her leg to pee on one of the oversized letters. "*That's* for whoever wrote that horrible review in *The Tribune!*" she'd howl. But it's also a scent that reminds me of screaming matches in the kitchen and a pot of boiling rigatoni overflowing on the stovetop with a *hsss*.

"Fine," I relent, allowing Ramón to pull me along. "But when I get back, you'd better not be here."

The MGM boardroom is warm, the entire easterly wall made of glass. I want to complain about my sweater—I'm sweltering—but Ramón looks as though he's eaten a lemon. His face is pinched and pale.

"Dominic Valentine," Jack Felton exclaims when he enters the room, a lit cigar in hand. He's wearing navy slacks that are slightly too long and a white button-down with shirt garters just above his elbows. "I've been hearing a lot about you this month." He sits on the opposite side of the long mahogany table, bluish smoke wafting above his toupee. I open my mouth to reply, but Ramón steps on my foot beneath the table.

Another man—thin, with swollen bags under his eyes—enters the room, carrying a thick folder. He sits to Jack's right. "I'm Reginald Hart, MGM's lawyer," he says, producing a pen from his breast pocket. Ramón stiffens beside me. I can nearly feel the anxiety oozing off him, as thick and as rank as sludge. The lawyer being present is effectively a shot across my bow—a threat.

Jack, Reginald, and Ramón stare at me. I desperately want to make a joke. *Did you hear about the cat who swallowed a ball of yarn?*

Finally, Jack continues. "Do you have anything to say for yourself?"

Ramón nearly leaps out of his chair, eager to respond. "Sir, can I remind you that my client has made MGM tens of millions of dollars, just on name recognition alone? His last three films have been number one in the box office, and he's been featured in *Variety* on—"

Jack raises a hand, rendering my friend mute. "I was speaking to Dominic."

"I'm not sure what you want me to say, Jack," I reply. "What have you heard?" Beneath the table, Ramón grinds his heel into my foot.

"That you pick fights with directors and costars. That you show up whenever you feel like, often inebriated or hungover. You effectively delayed the release of *Cattlemen* by six months." The lawyer scribbles something on a yellow legal pad, showing it to the executive. "And, apparently, Kubrick never wants to work with you again."

"To be fair, sir, no one wants to work with Kubrick either." I lean back in my chair, slinging my arm over the chairback. I know I should be contrite or, at least, act as though I am. But they have put me on the offensive. Naturally, I'm going to bare my teeth. Surely, they expected nothing less.

"As you know, we have a contract with you for two more years," Jack continues, ignoring my quip. "Your agent is right; audiences adore you. But you are on thin ice, Valentine. And believe me when I say: if we have to void your contract, we will make sure you never work in this town again."

"Are you threatening to blacklist me?" In the last five years, the Blacklist has become Hollywood's Boogeyman, swallowing up even those deemed untouchable like Charlie Chaplin and Orson Welles. Often, a rumor of Communist leanings was more than enough ammunition. *Did you hear? Charlie is a Bolshevik. My friend said that* Citizen Kane *is a smear campaign against capitalism!* Surely, MGM could find the tiniest sliver of evidence against me. *Dominic Valentine's favorite color is RED!*

"We don't have to threaten you," Jack replies coolly. "It's a promise." His steely eyes bore into mine. I am suddenly cognizant of a prickling at the base of my neck, an itching sensation upon my palms. I clench my fists in my lap, my nails cutting jagged quarter moons into my skin. I want to leap across the table and slam Jack's face into the knotted mahogany until he's little more than pulp.

Abruptly switching gears, Jack grins, clapping his hands together. "Now, let's talk about your next picture." He gestures to the lawyer, who pushes a sheaf of paper toward me. It's a film contract, a red X scrawled where I'm supposed to sign.

I make no move to pick them up, so Ramón reaches for them. "'*Don't Look in the Lake*'," he reads aloud, "'start date: June 18, 1951.'"

"It's a horror picture directed by Otto Lang," Jack clarifies. "You'll play a scientist who becomes a monster."

I guffaw, forgetting the guillotine dangling above my neck. "Really? A horror movie? You're joking." I'd almost rather he called Joseph McCarthy personally and said I was in bed with Stalin! At least then my demise would be over quickly. Instead, he's shown me a future where I will make schlocky B-movies until I become a laughingstock or, worse, a *character actor.*

"He'll do it," Ramón says, aiming a kick at my shin. "Of course, he'll do it."

Chapter Three
(FLORA)

————◁◆▷————

Carter Merlotte saws at his ham steak, pork grease glistening upon his lips. "How are your boiled eggs?"

I stare at the two smooth half-spheres on my plate, the yolks as yellow as a caution sign. A triangle of plain wheat toast rests alongside them. Mr. Merlotte ordered for me. "Fine," I reply glumly, staring longingly at his sumptuous meal.

"Marilyn Monroe orders the same thing every morning," he says, oblivious. "Don't forget to drink your coffee. It's good for your figure." He spears his poached egg with the tines of his fork, creamy yolk flooding his plate and lapping against his own triangle of toast topped with a thick layer of butter and jam. "How are you feeling about your audition this afternoon?"

Last night, I studied the two-page script Ingrid left in my hotel room until my eyes grew heavy. There was very little context for the scene; the pages had clearly been pulled from a much longer script. My character, Daphne Page, is looking for her husband in their sprawling mansion but finds a hideous monster instead. The snarling beast advances upon her, and she cowers, brandishing a fireplace poker. The only lines underlined involve hysterical simpering, "Leave me alone!"

"I've never had to cry on cue," I reply honestly.

"I know a lot of actresses who think of something horrible that happened to them," Mr. Merlotte says before loudly slurping his glass of orange juice and, I suspect, champagne. "Surely, you can think of something."

He's had three drinks so far, rudely snapping at the harried waitress when he runs low. It's apparent he eats at the hotel's ballroom frequently. The staff address him by name, and I can't help but notice the nervous wobble when they ask, "What can I help you with, sir?"

"And," he continues, "if you get the part, Otto Lang will make sure you cry when he wants you to cry. He's very talented in that way."

"Oh?" I take a sip of my coffee, wrinkling my nose at the bitter taste. I asked the waitress for cream and sugar, but Mr. Merlotte waved her away as though she was a mosquito.

"Did you see *Crazed*? He was the one who made Sheila Dumonte win the Academy Award."

I have seen it. In one particular scene, Sheila Dumonte cries so hard that her mascara runs and coats her upper lip; her sobs double her over, as if in immense pain. I don't think I want to know how he elicited that performance from her. I'm relieved my stomach is empty. Otherwise, I might vomit in fear. I push my plate away.

Mr. Merlotte nods approvingly and orders another drink.

In the afternoon, Ingrid drives me to the audition space—a nondescript warehouse with no signage out front. But inside, it is apparent what the building is for. The reception area is crowded, chock full of women who could be my long-lost sisters. We are all of similar height, build, and complexion. Clearly, the casting call was very specific. It makes me feel all the more uneasy. I will never be able to stand out.

Ingrid signs me in, and we find a bit of bare wall upon which to lean. "Did you hear?" she asks, having to lean close. Most of the hopefuls are practicing their lines aloud.

"Did I hear what?" I ask, the script wrinkling in my fidgeting hands. I feel clammy, and I worry I'm going to be ill.

"The leading man has already been cast. It's Dominic Valentine." She whispers his name, drawing out the vowels into a purr.

"Isn't he known for being hard to work with?" I've read a few articles in *Photoplay* magazine in which his exploits have been featured. Often, a modeling photo accompanied the article, drawing attention to his dark features and arrogant smile.

"He's known for being a Casanova," Ingrid says with a laugh. "He dates everyone he works with.

Everyone thought he was going to settle down with Penelope Cox, but that didn't last long."

Penelope Cox's name is like a lance through my ribs. She's uber-famous, starring in at least half of the big-budget films released in the last five years. She is touted as a more accessible Marilyn Monroe, not lacking sex appeal but employing it in a less overt way than the Blond Bombshell. While Marilyn wears short dresses and offers the viewer a tantalizing glimpse of her milky thighs, Penelope Cox wears pantsuits with plunging necklines that reveals the flat plane of her sternum and the shadows of her breasts. I've been following her career closely and ferreting away her Lancôme ads. I'm not sure if I want to be her or kiss her.

"He was with Penelope Cox?" I ask, unable to hide the tremble in my voice. I never thought I would be rubbing elbows with someone who rubbed *more* than elbows with my idol.

Ingrid nods. "It was as brief and as *loud* as a mortar. There are rumors it is still on-again-off-again, depending on the way the wind is blowing."

Suddenly, a door opens, and a man with a clipboard lingers in the doorway. As if one entity, the hopeful actresses turn to look, as silent as though they've entered a church sanctuary. "Next up: Flora Wright," he calls.

"Break a leg," Ingrid whispers, nudging me forward. Rooted to the spot, I merely sway. *I can't do this.* Then Ingrid gives me another push, her palm driving into the small of my back.

Reluctantly, I follow the man into the private room. It's small and windowless, with a table at the far end.

Two men and a woman sit there and stare as though I'm a circus animal about to do a trick. I suppose that is accurate. "Hello," I manage, suddenly cognizant of how unwieldy my tongue is in my mouth.

"Flora Wright, correct?" the woman asks.

"Yes, ma'am." I stand just before the table, smoothing imaginary wrinkles from my dress. *Can they tell I'm sweating?* I imagine dark, wet patches beneath my arms and breasts, turning my navy dress black.

"You may begin," she says, twirling her pen between her long, nimble fingers.

"Yes, ma'am," I repeat. I try, in vain, to think of my lines, but it's as though they've flown away, leaving me with a vague jumble of words that don't quite make sense. The woman sighs loudly.

One of the men at the table clears his throat then reads the action portion of the script in a smooth-as-caramel drawl. "'It is storming. Daphne Page heads down to the basement to look for her husband, George. Midway down the stairs, the power goes out, plunging her into complete darkness. At the bottom of the stairs, she finds a flashlight on the shelf and uses it to scan the room. Then, she sees the monster.'"

"What! W-w-what are you?" I stammer, surprised at the fear in my voice. I *am* frightened—just not of a monster.

The man reads George's line, pitching his voice down. "'Daphne, it's me.'"

"Leave me alone!" I shriek, taking three stumbling steps backward. "Stay back!" I throw a hand out as if to protect myself from an attack. In the script, the monster tries to touch the hysterical housewife, and she fights him off with a fireplace poker, runs up the stairs, and slams the door. But here, it's just me and my costar. I haven't even been offered a prop.

"'Daphne locks the door and falls back against it, sobbing.'"

Feeling a little foolish, I run to the door through which I entered and mime opening it wide and slamming it shut. Then, I slump against it, panting.

You have to cry.

Mr. Merlotte said to summon a sad thought. Ingrid said to break a leg. Perhaps acting is no more than subjecting oneself to little tortures, like pulling fingernails up one-by-one. It's not all that dissimilar from turning wolfish; one must embrace the pain and accept that they will no longer be alone in their own head. I must become Daphne much like I become the red wolf.

I think of a photo I recently found in the Cove's front office, tucked into a drawer under a decades' worth of tax returns and receipts from contractors. It was a photo Samuel took years ago while Rafe was overseas: Nico and Elton sitting poolside, their arms draped over each other's shoulders. Finding it was like a kick to the chest. All of the air left my lungs, and I nearly lost my balance, gripping the counter. I was struck by how young Nico was in the photo. He was only twenty when he died, but it was easy to forget that he was just a child. He always acted so grown up. Elton was smiling in the photo, his bristly cheek squished against Nico's. I could see all of his teeth— the same teeth he would use to rip Nico apart.

Tears trickle down my cheeks, and a sob erupts from between my quivering lips. Soon, I am bawling.

The woman sitting at the table says, "Cut."

CHAPTER FOUR
(DOMINIC)

The Hollywood elite take great care to avoid their adoring public. We spend much of our time skulking around industrial spaces, the no man's land between the glitz8y galas and the rat-infested alleyways. It's simpler than facing the flash-bulbs ("Dominic! Look over here!") and the tears of hyperventilating teens, clamoring for an autograph ("Dominic, I love you!")

Ramón parks beside the Amherst building's loading dock, and we climb the rickety stairs leading into the industrial kitchen. A homeless man sits beneath the stairs atop an Army surplus sleeping bag, and I try very hard to avoid his eyes.

The kitchen hasn't been used in some time. A fine layer of dust coats the stainless-steel countertops, and a cobweb dangles from the u-shaped faucet. I balk just before the double doors, but Ramón grasps my elbow, propelling me through them. "We're late," he reminds me testily.

The Amherst building is a studio space, and each time I'm here, it looks different. Currently, the building looks to be wearing the facade of a corporate space. Except, the walls are paper thin and don't quite touch the ductwork on the 10-foot ceilings. Someone had hung framed MGM film posters. I feature prominently. I spot the promotional images for *Cattlemen, Freezer Burn*, and *Changing Seasons* placed equidistant from each other. I wonder if the posters were hung to stroke my ego.

"Mr. Valentine, good of you to finally join us." A man stands in the narrow hallway, a steaming cup of coffee in hand. He looks like a Teamster, dressed in the typical uniform of the quintessential blue-collar worker—Levi's, a baseball cap, an unshaven jaw, a permanent slouch, and the blank expression of the perpetually bored. He certainly doesn't look like someone with the stature to chide the talent. He sticks his hand out to shake. "Otto Lang," he says by way of introduction.

"Otto Lang, the *director?*" I ask. I had assumed he would have a more Hitchcockian air to him. In fact, I had pictured a straight-backed, moody man with a penchant for English suits. Lang is the antithesis of that in every conceivable way. In fact, I would describe him as "sloppy."

"The one and only," he replies coolly. "You were meant to be here an hour ago. The actresses had the decency to show up on time." The difference between myself and my potential costars is that I already have the job while they're still in competition. "Let's get started, shall we?" He gestures toward one of the many nondescript doors with his half-empty coffee cup.

The room is fairly large, with a small makeshift film stage on one end. It's dressed to resemble a living room, with a couch and a television set. The latter is made of painted cardboard. A single camera is trained on the couch, and three lights illuminate the space: a key light, a filler light, and a backlight.

Otto beckons for me to step onto the raised platform. "Let's not waste any more time," he says shortly.

I find the taped "x" on the floor, rolling my shoulders. I would have preferred to have a cup of coffee first, or to peruse the craft services table, but Otto is clearly not in the mood. "How many screen tests are we filming?" I ask as he settles into the canvas chair near the camera.

"Only two," he replies. He turns to a lingering assistant. "Can you fetch our first lucky lady?" She nods and hurries into a side room, her heels tapping a staccato on the concrete floor.

Ramón sidles over to the table laden with snacks and selects a bagel. He offers me a thumbs up before taking an enormous bite. I hope he gets poppy seeds in his beard.

The assistant returns from a side room, a woman in tow. With the filler light pouring into my eyes, I can't quite make out her features. "Flora," Otto says, "please take your mark."

The woman steps up onto the set, finding the other "x" on the floor. For a brief moment, she meets my eyes, offering me a tight smile. She looks nervous, her lower lip quivering spasmodically. Her hands tense and relax at her sides.

We stand several feet apart, a coffee table laden with books between us. Clearly, the set dresser wasn't picky—the books range from Carnegie's *How to Stop Worrying & Start Living* to a car maintenance manual.

"Quiet on set," Otto calls. "Roll sound. Camera ready?"

"Ready," chirps the camera operator, his eye pressed against the viewfinder. He adjusts the angle so the lens is trained on the actress.

The assistant who retrieved the actress hops on set, clapboard in hand. "Screen test, Flora Wright, take one. Mark!" she announces, clapping the ticks together. The sound makes the actress—*Flora*—jump.

"Action," Otto adds.

I look expectantly at Flora. She has the first line. In the light, she looks a little green. With any luck, she'll pass out and I can go home early. I am already feeling less than agreeable after Otto Lang's cold shoulder.

But then, she blurts out, "George, it's as though you don't see me. I'm thinking of going to my mother's..."

She delivers the line too fast and without emotion. Daphne is meant to be distraught, upset at her husband. Conversely, her husband is meant to console her, to chip at her resolve. She cannot leave the mansion when he's so close to a breakthrough. "Daph," I croon, "please, listen—"

Flora crosses her arms over her chest as I skirt around the table, resting my hands on her bunched shoulders. At my touch, her skin jumps. "You've had your nose in your books, spent whole nights in your study. It's as though I don't exist." Her voice is soft, perhaps too soft for the hovering boom mics to pick up.

I'm meant to kiss her now. It's the reason Lang chose this scene for the test. He wants his leads to have palatable chemistry, like Fred Astaire and Ginger Rogers, Clark Gable and Gene Harlow, or Katherine Hepburn and Spencer Tracy. It's the backbone of the film.

Her breath quickens as I lean close. Suddenly, I am cognizant of her scent—wild like the wind whipping off the Pacific, woodsy and balsamic like sandalwood. It's the smell of wolf pelt, damp from a springtime downpour.

What was my line again?

"If you weren't here, I wouldn't exist. I would just be the monster you think I am," I finally muster. Then, I wrap my hand around the back of her neck, pulling her mouth toward mine. Her lips part just slightly, and—

"Cut!" Otto calls. Flora and I freeze, our breath commingling. "Let's get Leena out here next!" Flora's eyes flick toward the director then back toward me before she breaks our embrace.

Can she smell me too?

The restaurant at the Chateau Marmont is typically crowded, every conceivable inch occupied by celebrities and their hangers-on. But my patio table is free, a "reserved" placard at its center. A plate of nibbles is already waiting for us, piled high with my favorites. A bottle of Crémant de Luxembourg chills tableside.

"Who do you think will get the part?" Ramón asks, shoveling a forkful of black truffle arancini into his mouth. I'm not sure how he can bear to eat a single bite. Each time I caught his eye during the screen test, he was eating a cube of cheese or a tea sandwich, licking his fingers like a toddler. He grazed the craft services table with the same gusto as a goat chomping on poison ivy.

"It's Leena's part to lose," I reply easily, thinking of the wisp of a woman who followed Flora. We've worked together before. She played my sister in *Cattlemen*, and we have chemistry in spades; our woefully brief, albeit passionate, relationship on the balmy Badlands set is the proof in the pudding. I wouldn't be averse to reigniting that particular flame again, preferably in a more temperate locale.

"I'm not so sure about that," Ramón muses. "There was passion there, sure. But it was nothing compared to the chemistry between you and Flora. It looked like you were going to *swallow her whole.*"

The waitress brings our entrees: hangar steak salad for me and spaghetti bolognese for Ramón. I wait for her to refill our glasses with wine and wish us *bon appetit* before leaning conspiratorially toward my friend. "Didn't you smell her?" I murmur. "Flora is one of us."

Ramón twirls his fork in his heaping serving of pasta, the tagliatelle noodles winding around the tines. The sauce turns his pale lips crimson. "Is she? Do you think we've come across her before? While wolfish, I mean." Los Angeles is a hub city, and many of the wolves we meet out in the brush are nomadic,

31

occupying that moment of stasis between coming and going. All it takes is one failed audition or relation-ship for a wolf to leave our pack without so much as a goodbye. In a sense, L.A is "home *for now*" for all of us. Even my star could blink out eventually, exiling me back to Texas.

"Not a chance." I pop a strip of medium-rare steak into my mouth and chew. "She was so nervous, as though she just hopped off the plane from bumfuck nowhere." Myoglobin trickles down my chin, and I wipe it away with my knuckles.

"I've seen you shoot a lot of scenes with a lot of women—and men too," Ramón muses. "But today, with her? That was unreal. Otto is going to hire her for that alone. Can you imagine the press?"

"Surely, it wasn't that apparent." I take a sip of my wine, the crisp tartness settling on the back of my tongue. "Besides, she could hardly get the lines out. Otto would be stupid to hire her. It would be a waste of his time—mine too."

CHAPTER FIVE
(FLORA)

—◁◆▷—

When she enters my hotel room, Ingrid is a dervish. Her skinny arms laden with Hermés, Balenciaga, and Christian Dior shopping bags, she nearly bowls me over when I open the door. "You got the part!" she crows, dropping her parcels onto the glass tabletop. A semi-circular hatbox rolls out of one, nearly colliding with my half-finished cup of black coffee. She doesn't seem to notice, her cheeks a vibrant rouge.

"I did?" I had bitten my nails to the quick while fretting about last week's audition. In my mind, it had gone horribly. After meeting Dominic Valentine, I could hardly squeak out my lines. He smelled like petrichor and ozone, as ominous as a slow-rolling thunderstorm. It made me feel off-balance, as though the earth's tectonic plates had shifted beneath me—and only me. I remember looking out at Otto Lang and his staff, wanting to ask, "Do you feel that?"

"We have a few weeks before principal photography begins," Ingrid continues, "and we have a lot of work to do in the meantime."

I sink into one of the high-backed dining room chairs, resting my palms on the cool tabletop. "Are you sure this isn't a mistake?" Surely, it has to be. I saw a few moments of Leena Marvell's screen test, and she was incredible, confidence oozing from her pores.

Ingrid laughs, elbow-deep in one of the shopping bags. "Carver has been on the phone for hours with MGM and Mr. Lang. Trust me. You have the job." She pulls out a canary yellow gown with a poufy skirt and holds it against my bosom. "This will look perfect."

"For what, exactly?" I feel like I'm ten steps behind her with no hope of catching up. I feel breathless.

"Carver wants to get your face out there. You're going to the premiere of *Rear Window* tomorrow. We're negotiating contracts with Emilio Pucci and Elizabeth Arden to get you some commercial campaigns."

"I've never been to a movie premiere," I manage, staring at my reflection on the tabletop. I look pale and pinched—sickly. I can almost feel the coffee sloshing in my belly, the waves rolling under and over each other—my own personal Black Sea.

"You sound like you've been asked to go to a church burning, Flora," Ingrid scolds me. "This is meant to be fun. Besides, I'll be with you, guiding you every step of the way. But we have to hurry and pack. The premiere is in New York."

Broadway is congested with sleek vehicles, idling head- to taillight. Car exhaust makes the air shimmer as though we are entering a mirage. We may as well be; I've never seen anything like the Rivoli Theatre with its marquee ablaze, the cavalcade of paparazzi lining the street. Every few moments, our car moves up another few feet in the queue, and flashbulbs erupt.

"We're next," Ingrid says. "Remember, smile." The car shudders forward, and Ingrid climbs out, stepping aside to let me through. Taking a deep breath, I follow her out onto the red carpet. I catch only a glimpse of the cameras before the flashbulbs blind me. *Smile!* I remind myself. After the shutters close, it takes me a moment to get my bearings again, and I take my first tentative step.

I vaguely hear the paparazzi shouting at whom-ever has pulled up in the next car, but I'm too focused on moving toward the theatre's entrance. Nightmares of tripping over my dress plagued me throughout the entire red eye flight, and I can't have them come true. In my nightmares, the embarrassment caused my fur to burst forth, my violently contorting body tearing the gown into ribbons.

Suddenly, a large hand cups the small of my back. At first, I think it's Ingrid, telling me I've messed up. *Have I forgotten to smile?* No, I haven't; my cheeks hurt terribly. "Well, if it isn't Flora Wright," a deep baritone murmurs, a hint of an accent making his words sound somehow both flowery and sneering.

Dominic Valentine doesn't look at me, his dark eyes on the paparazzi. He smiles, showing every one of his perfect teeth. "Your team planned this, didn't they?" he murmurs out of the corner of his mouth. I'm not sure what he's talking about.

A reporter jabs a microphone between us, asking rapid fire questions. "Dominic, are you here tonight with Ms. Wright? We hear you two are shooting a movie with Otto Lang directing. What can you tell us about it?"

"I can't wait for you to see Otto's vision. Like *Rear Window*, it's a horror picture, but at its heart, it's a love story," Dominic replies easily. He grins at me, though the light of it doesn't quite reach his eyes. "Mark my words: Flora here will be a household name."

"You make a lovely couple," the reporter says. "It's quite the whirlwind romance, isn't it?"

Dominic's jaw tightens, and the hand upon my back spasms. "We'd better get inside," he says, his voice even. "Come along, *dear*." Before the reporter can ask anything else, Dominic steers me into the theatre's cool lobby. It's crowded with would-be movie-goers, nary a camera in-sight. Dominic turns to face me, nostrils flaring. "You have some nerve, kid."

"I don't know what you're talking about," I stammer. I look for Ingrid's coiffed platinum hairdo in the crowd but don't immediately spot her. *Where is she?*

"Your car arriving just before mine. The article in *Confidential*. Really, Flora?"

"What article?" I don't have any idea what he's talking about. I've spent the last twenty-four hours in Ingrid's tailwind: trying on dresses, sitting through makeup and hair trials, and white-knuckling my way through another intercontinental flight.

"Apparently, we're having a secret affair," Dominic says with a snicker. "But surely, you knew that already.

It's pathetic." He nearly spits the last word, the final consonant causing him to bare his square teeth.

The lights in the lobby flicker, letting the loiterers know that *Rear Window* is about to start. Dominic shoots me one more sour look before turning on his heel and stomping inside. Rudderless, I sway as the well-dressed crowd sweeps around me like a cattail moved by the current. Finally, Ingrid loops her arm with mine. "You left me," I mumble.

"The tabloids will be talking about you two for weeks," she squeals, as though we are two girlfriends sharing a secret.

"Did you have something to do with that?" I hiss, as we walk into the dim theatre. I catch a glimpse of Dominic in an aisle seat midway up the risers, his ankle resting casually upon his knee. He avoids my gaze as we climb past, turning to speak to the tuxedoed man sitting beside him.

"Carver's idea. Wasn't it genius? Nothing gets people more excited than a love story." We find our seats very near the back of the theatre between a man who smells like cigars and a woman with a persistent sniffle. From my vantage point, I can still see the back of Dominic's head.

"Dominic was upset. He thinks I'm using him," I say just before the audience erupts in applause. Alfred Hitchcock steps onto the stage, Grace Kelly and James Stewart flanking him like a retinue. As the esteemed director takes the microphone, clearing his throat, Ingrid leans close to murmur into my ear.

"This is Hollywood; everyone uses each other."

CHAPTER SIX
(OTTO)

———◁◆▷———

"What do you think?" Mitchell Emerson asks, slapping a hand on the mannequin's shoulder. It's less stable than he thinks, and it nearly topples to the ground. He steadies it by grasping its tapered waist. For an instant, he looks like he's awkwardly posing for a photo with a date. The adult acne on his cheeks lends itself to the overall image.

The costume is terrifying. The monster—*my* monster—looks just as I imagined. Its eyeholes are empty, revealing the mannequin's plasticky flesh beneath. It is covered in green fur and kelp, an amalgamation of the *Wolf-Man* and the eponymous *Creature from the Black Lagoon*. I poke at the monster's short rubber snout, revealing the painted-on teeth beneath its pliant lips.

"What about the arms? The hands?" I ask. At present, the costume consists of only a mask and a torso. It's supposed to cover the actor from head to toe.

Mitchell bends at the waist to paw through a cardboard box. "The guys made two versions. They weren't sure which you'd like more." He pulls the gloves on, flexing his fingers. The left is humanoid, webbing between each digit, fingers tipped with a scythe-like claw. The right is more akin to a paw, a dewclaw adorning the wrist. Mitchell turns his hand to show me the paw pads on the palm. They are calloused and cracked as though the monster dragged himself through a swamp.

"This one doesn't exactly strike fear, does it?" Mitchell asks, holding up his right hand. "It makes the monster look like Rin-Tin-Tin."

But I'm thinking of the paw print beneath the oak tree, the howls of the men-turned-wolves outside my cabin door. I'm thinking of the feverish way I wrote *Don't Look in the Lake!* in the days following, too frightened to sleep, popping amphetamines to keep my heavy eyelids at half-mast. If I fell asleep, I was certain they would come back for me. "They'll be iconic," I counter.

"It's *your* picture, boss," Mitchell relents, shrugging as if to say *it's no skin off my fucking nose, pal.* "The prop guys will make feet to match. Would you like the monster to have a tail too?"

After the meeting with Mitchell Emerson, I head toward Studio H. I can hear the cacophony of hammers striking nails from down the block. The set designers squawk at one another over the radio, using their own secret language. "Make sure to put asphaltum on that banister! Where's my ditty bag? I am not liking the mise en scène with the lighting here—there are too many highlights. It's not a horror film if you can see *everyfuckingthing*!"

Studio H is a whirlwind of activity. It's the site of all the film's indoor scenes, and several stages have to be constructed before principal photography begins next week. I pass what will eventually be the mansion's basement and foyer before climbing the rickety stairs to my office space. It's little more than a supply closet in which I've wedged a desk and a chair. The desk is covered in books with titles like *The Legend of Lycaon*, *The Bedburg Werewolf*, *The Epic of Gilgamesh*, and *Burgot and Verdun*.

All of the books include references to men who turned into wolves through either curse or circumstance. Surely, the intruders in Black Star Canyon couldn't have been flesh-and-blood men! Where had the paw print come from? What made the blood-curdling howls? Surely, human vocal cords are incapable!

I pore over the tomes when I'm supposed to be doing script rewrites. Most are quite old, pilfered from the prop department's storeroom. Books from estate sales and antique stores look the best on-screen and, I find, have a more serious bent when it comes to werewolves. In the good ol' days, people let themselves believe in the fantastical, didn't they?

I shuffle through the books and pick one at random. It's leatherbound, as thin as a tract, with the title embossed in gold leaf: *The Cure for Lycanthropy*. The first page is a woodcut print of a man with sharp teeth, his tongue too thick and lolling to remain in his mouth. He is naked and pierced by hundreds of arrows

oozing black blood. A halo of fire surrounds his contorted body, his limbs at right angles.

*A man with lycanthropy is dangerous.
He will have an insatiable hunger for
human flesh—particularly that of children. Take, for instance, the case of the
hermit Giles Garnier, who confessed
to the murder of four children in the
French countryside. He craved the suc-
culent meat of their thighs and belly.*

*A wolfish man is not bound to any
convention. Neither the moon, the tides,
nor the clothes on his back cause his
transfiguration. Wolves are wolves
when they'd like to be. Garnier stated
that he was given a magical ointment
that caused his transformation, but
authorities never located the salve,
nor did any of the fifty witnesses at
his trial see him slathering it upon his
naked flesh.*

*The wolfish man is hungry—insa-
tiably so. He will kill indiscriminately
to sustain himself. Children are in the
greatest danger, but a wolfish man can
easily dispatch an unarmed adult.*

*Because they can appear human, a
wolfish man is difficult to spot. Some*

*sources say they will have a unibrow
or widow's peak, a ring finger longer
than their middle finger, irrational
fears (like, for instance, water or the
full moon), aggressive tendencies, and/
or reflective eyes.*

*You must kill the wolfish man, or he
will surely consume you. Garnier was
burned at the stake. However, other
methods of euthanasia are just as
effective including: a bullet through
the heart or brain, removal of the head,
poisoning, asphyxiation, cutting of the
throat or major arteries, et cetera.*

"Mr. Lang?" A man with a work belt slung around
his hips peeks into my office. I jump as though I've
been caught doing something untoward like snorting
a line of cocaine off my desk.

I shove the book beneath the desk, embarrassed.
But the man doesn't seem to notice my strange choice
of reading material. "You're needed downstairs. They
aren't sure where to hang the fresnel light."

"I'll be down in a minute," I mutter, avoiding
looking too carefully at the workman. I fear that I'll
spot bushy eyebrows or sharp canines. Everyone
feels like an enemy right now. *It's the amphetamines*,
I remind myself. *You're paranoid and exhausted*.
Before heading downstairs, I push the books into a
drawer. *Reading this filth isn't helping either*.

CHAPTER SEVEN
(DOMINIC)

---◁◆▷---

The makeup trailer is humid, the oscillating fan doing little to disperse the stagnant air. The towels tucked into my shirt collar are already damp with sweat. The makeup artist flits around the cramped space, applying layer after layer of powder to my face. She keeps apologizing for the heat as though it's her fault.

The trailer door squeals as Ramón pushes it open, climbing up the steep stairs. He's holding the call sheet, the MGM lion roaring just above the movie title and my name. "You have five minutes," he says, flopping into the second makeup chair. His long, stick-like legs get in the artist's way, and she scowls at him.

"We would have been done already if Lang sprung for an air-conditioned trailer," I mutter, glaring at my reflection in the mirror. My skin looks cakey and a shade too dark. I'm tempted to wipe the makeup off, but I am certain the makeup artist will burst into tears. She's already sniffling.

"First call is on the foyer set," Ramón says, examining the call sheet. "'Daphne and George have a sweet moment,' it says."

"Oh, I'm sure Flora will *love* that. It pushes her agenda." I roll my eyes, pulling the towels out of my collar and tossing them onto the worktop.

"You know how this business is, Dom. It's not the first time an actress has used you to get a leg up," Ramón reminds me. He's right; several women have called the paparazzi on themselves before doing the walk of shame out of my mansion, their hair coquettishly mussed. One even gossiped about our so-called "relationship" on *The Ed Sullivan Show*.

"At least those women had the decency to fuck me first" The makeup artist—who has taken great care to seem as though she isn't eavesdropping—gasps at my crass language and abruptly excuses herself. The door of the trailer crashes behind her, making the flimsy walls shake.

Ramón fishes a flask out of his suit jacket and hands it to me. "Buck up, champ." I take a gulp without asking what's inside, wrinkling my nose at the piney flavor. It's gin made lukewarm by Ramón's body heat. I take another gulp nonetheless. I'll need it to make it through today.

With my extremities warm and tingling, Ramón and I head into the studio space. The foyer set is easy to find—we only have to follow the sound of Otto Lang's shouting. As we round the corner, I see him standing midway up the foyer steps to nowhere, screaming at a production assistant.

"This is so fucking shoddy," he snarls, grabbing the banister and giving it a furious shake. It's clearly not well-made. A nail, pulled loose from its mooring, hits the plywood floor with a *plink!* "I don't give a shit whether you're union or not. This is not acceptable! I am not putting my actors on this death trap."

Flora is standing in the makeshift foyer too, her face pale. Her makeup artist was more adept than mine. With cheeks buffed to a lustrous pink, dewy eyelids, and eyebrows filled with a dark pencil to enhance their natural arch, she presses her glossy lips together, warily watching Otto tromp up and down the rickety half-staircase.

"Can't we just be here on the ground?" I ask, drawing their attention. "The staircase could be a backdrop."

"The *door* was meant to be the backdrop," Otto huffs, gesturing at the French doors with their stained-glass windows. "The camera was supposed to shoot downward, from mid-stair, with you two on the pen-ultimate step. Or did you not read the call sheet?"

I didn't, but he doesn't need to know that.

"I'm willing to risk falling down just two stairs if the whole lot collapses," I say. *With any luck, I'll break a leg and can bow out of this picture.* "How about you, Princess?"

Flora wrinkles her nose at the sobriquet, crossing her arms over her chest. "Perhaps you should let the *director* decide what he would like to do," she grumbles.

Otto looks half-crazed, his jaw working as though he's chewing an invisible wad of gum. It's as though he has been on a bender, and I should know, having been on many myself. It may be my imagination—or perhaps the artificial lighting streaming through the stained glass—but his nostrils look raw and red. I imagine him snorting a fat line of cocaine off his desk before traipsing down from his office up on the cat-walk. I'm not sure he should be making any decisions at all. This is not the creative genius the MGM executives described to me.

"Let's do a rehearsal on the stairs," Otto relents. "Try not to fall off. We're going to be behind schedule otherwise."

He clomps down the stairs and onto the floor, directing the cameraman up on the pneumatic lift to frame the shot from above. I step up two stairs, careful not to touch the unsound bannister. Flora hesitates but joins me on the bottom step. She carefully adjusts her skirt, her eyes on the camera's dark lens.

"Action," Otto says from beyond the studio lights. A clatter follows the order; he's dropped something. Faint curses follow.

"George," Flora says, her voice much less shaky than it was during our screen test. "This big old house—surely, it's too much for us." Despite the improvement, her eyes have the unfocused quality of someone who is mentally elsewhere. She's picturing the script, not the scene unfolding in front of her.

"Perhaps," I reply easily, "but haven't you pictured it? Imagine how this house will sound filled with children—our children!" This is meant to be a revelation to Flora's character. After all, Daphne is the long-suffering wife of a workaholic, and a family has always seemed unattainable to her. Her husband's retort to the question of children has always been *someday, eventually, after the next breakthrough, I promise.* Promises lose their weight after a while.

"Do you mean it?" she breathes, reaching for my hands. "Really, George?" I wait for her eyes to grow round, to search my face as if divining my—George's—intentions. But her expression is neutral. I can almost see her turning the script pages in her mind's eye, lips pursed as she waits to deliver her next line.

I roll my eyes, wrenching my hands away and stepping off my mark. Flora blinks dumbly at me. "W-where are you going?" she stammers.

"I can't work like this," I reply, my tone scathing. "It's like acting opposite a fucking *mannequin.*" I step off the raised set, stabbing my finger into Otto Lang's bony sternum as I pass. "You really made the wrong choice with this little girl, Lang."

Before Otto can respond, Flora flies off the set like a dervish, hackles raised. Her skirt flares around her ankles. "You have a lot of nerve, Dominic Valentine!" She nearly collides with me in her haste, spitting like an agitated cat. "You've been horribly unprofessional since the minute we've met."

"I've been doing this job for well over two decades. *You* can barely deliver a simple line. Talk to me about professionalism after you've been here a year—if you even make it that far."

The smell of petrichor and lemongrass fills my nostrils, and her eyes flash. "I'm trying my best," she snarls. I want to push her further, to make those pretty teeth go sharp. Let them all see what she is. A tickling sensation edges up my spine, and I clench my fists to hide my thickening nail beds.

"Well, your best isn't good enough. Maybe go back to community theater," I reply coolly. "I'm sure your little jerkwater town needs a witch for *The Crucible*."

Flora's nostrils flare. "I'm right where I'm supposed to be, Dominic. Surely, I wouldn't be here otherwise."

"Prove it."

Otto wedges himself between us, his red-tinged eyes on Flora. "This," he exclaims. "*This* is why I chose you. Channel this into Daphne. She's lonely in this enormous house and feeling as though she's been locked out of her husband's life. Offering up children is his idea of a *mea culpa*, but she's suspicious of his intentions. She has to look at George how you're looking at Dominic now."

Flora's eyes remain on my face, her eyebrows furrowed. Her lips press together so hard they turn white beneath her oily lipstick.

"Let's run the scene again," Otto says.

Reluctantly, we both take our places on the step. We avoid each other's eyes, though Flora's cheeks are burning.

Flora barely lets Otto get out "Action!" before she launches into her dialogue, her eyes wide and hopeful. "Do you mean it?" she says with a gasp, threading her fingers with mine. "Really, George?"

"Of course. It's what we've dreamed of, isn't it?"

"You're certain?" She takes a shaky step closer to me, looking up at my face. Her jaw sets just as it had when I insulted her, and her grip tightens.

"For you, my love, *anything*," I reply casually, knowing that for George, the lie will come easy. It's just another tossed upon the pile. Happy wife, happy life.

As soon as the scene ends ("Cut!") Flora hops off the staircase. "Perhaps you could try not to have a tantrum next time," she says airily.

CHAPTER EIGHT
(FLORA)

—◁◆▷—

The rain taps against the trailer's windowpane like a surreptitious lover vying for my attention. I press my cheek against the cool windowpane, staring out at the grey water of Bass Lake. The pine trees surrounding the shore droop, their needles heavily with rainwater. The lake churns, the dark water resembling mud. I imagine if I fell in, I'd never be able to find the surface again.

We've been trying to wait out the storm for hours now, desperate to film the scene where Daphne runs from her husband, falls into the water at the end of the pier, and then surfaces, sputtering, only to find him gone. The hairdresser has already braided bits of twig and a few leaves into my hair in preparation for the scene. One of the branches scrapes against the sensitive skin on my neck when I move my head to the right.

Someone knocks at my trailer door, and I answer it, expecting to see one of the many now-familiar faces that act as Otto's eyes and ears. Perhaps we are going to film despite the weather.

But it's Dominic, standing beneath an umbrella. "Oh," I say dumbly, not sure what to make of his presence. He hasn't made an effort to speak to me unless he's channeling George. Though, he's particularly adept at showing his disdain with just a look.

"Are you going to let me in?" he asks dryly. "It's raining cats and dogs."

I step back into the trailer so he can climb up the trio of steps. He closes his umbrella, leaving it to dribble water on the landing. "What are you doing here?" I ask as he brushes past me in the small space and takes a seat on the plush couch I had just left.

"I thought it best we have a talk." Dominic drapes his muscular arms over the back of the couch. He takes up most of the space, and if I sit, we will inevitably touch. Instead, I remain standing, crossing my arms over my chest.

"About what, exactly?"

"About your attitude," he says. "You are new here, so maybe you're still ignorant of how it works on set."

I scoff. Dominic Valentine is the king of having a piss poor attitude both on set and off. He often gets into shouting matches with Otto and has delayed filming on more than one occasion by refusing to leave his trailer.

Seemingly unaware of my annoyance, he continues, "You just aren't very respectful. You make stupid mistakes. If I had my way, you would be fired."

I guffaw. "I'm not respectful to *whom*?"

"Me," he answers impatiently. "I'm not sure what— or who—you did to get this role, but the least you can do is realize how lucky you are. You're going to make *millions* from working with me."

I snort. "Dominic, I have been nothing but kind toward you." The insinuation that I slept with someone to get this role makes me furious. Paresthesia trickles down my spine.

"Oh, yes, like when you told *Confidential* that we're dating. So kind!" He laughs, slapping at his knee.

"I told you I had nothing to do with that."

"They have quotes from you, kid," he says with a snicker. "Let me think. What did you say again? 'Dominic makes me feel so safe, and I am so happy that we get to work together, professionally.'"

"Clearly, I didn't say that," I counter. "You've had your teeth bared at me since the day we met."

Dominic Valentine abruptly rises from the couch. With both of us standing in the narrow aisle between the couch and the dinette, the sharp edge of his hip bone butts up against me. I try to take a half-step backward, but the edge of the dinette table jabs painfully into my spine. I'm effectively trapped. He takes my chin in his hand, his thumb peeling my lip away from my squarish teeth. "It's funny you mention teeth," he croons.

Suddenly, I am cognizant of something I wasn't before. It's not that I hadn't smelt him, but I had mistaken the scent of pine forests and freshly tilled soil with cologne. How else could it smell so strong? It boldly inundates my nostrils, shouldering aside all else: the sweetness of my cup of tea and milk, gone cold hours before; the chemical, synapse-sizzling smell of my hairspray; and even the acetone the makeup artist had used to buff my nails clean.

Dominic smiles, and his teeth are sharp, carnassial. The canine teeth curve just slightly, ending in wicked points. *All the better to rip you apart with, my dear!* In his human mouth, the teeth look inordinately large, crowding the limited space in a staggered formation, reminiscent of a shark's many rows. "It's rude not to announce yourself to the Alpha," he rasps, his cramped tongue unable to properly bend. His voice is deeper now, rumbling in my chest wall like a bass line at a concert.

"Everyone in this town is rude." My voice is markedly even despite his aggressive posturing. His closeness makes me feel off-balance, my weight in my heels. If it weren't for the table, I would topple over. I want to push him away, but he's far larger than me. It would only make him laugh. "Pardon me for not prostrating myself before you."

I've seen it before. Wolves who wander into Wharton proper find their way to Rafe sooner or later. It's as though they are swept into his riptide. Typically, they approach him at The Cove, hats in hands, eyes downcast. They call him "sir" and act contrite, as if they walked into a party without a gift. I've never experienced that drive, having been a Whartonite for my entire life, standing shoulder to shoulder with Rafe since we were snot-nosed pups with perpetually scraped knees. Despite his station, I never felt that the ground we stood on was uneven.

But here?

It is apparent that Dominic is not Rafe. He is nothing like my kind friend, who pats newcomers on the back and offers them a Coca-Cola from the vending machine. "Stay as long as you'd like," he'd say congenially. "Welcome to Virginia." He never threatened, nor showed his teeth. Not unless he was forced to.

"It's no matter," Dominic says, waving away my snide non-apology. "You won't be here long. It doesn't matter how sharp your teeth are. This town is going to chew you up. I just have to wait." With that, he steps away from me, heading toward the door. Frozen, I watch him swing open the door, thrust his umbrella into the storm, and pop it open with a flick of his wrist. Then, he's gone, tromping down the row of trailers to his own.

I sink down onto the couch, into the warm indent where his body once was. I can still smell him there, and it makes me agitated.

It's as though Hollywood is too bright, dulling all my other senses. I have inadvertently missed so much, too focused on screwing up my eyes to protect my retinas from the never-ending flashbulbs. I never saw Dominic for what he was. He's not just an arrogant man-child with a silver spoon wedged firmly between his teeth, but more powerful than anyone can possibly surmise.

And my agent isn't my protector or liaison. He threw me to the sharks like chum. The article that tied Dominic and me together is a clarion call to every other actress in the business. *Here she is: your new enemy.* *Confidential* described me as a country bumpkin who stumbled into this business and was handed the keys to the kingdom and the heart of the crown prince.

I miss Virginia. The thought bubbles up, unbidden, and crashes upon every synapse. It's as though my skin has sloughed off, leaving my nerves exposed to the open air. My skin prickles, the red wolf wanting to run East until her paws disintegrate into bloody stumps.

Chapter Nine
(OTTO)

---◁◆▷---

Thunder rolls over the temporary village of trailers, shaking the walls. There's no way we're shooting the scene today. Even if the rain should stop within the next few minutes, the ground would be slick for hours and the light would be *shit*.

It's almost six o'clock in the evening, and once the clouds clear, I expect the sun will be sitting quite low on the horizon line on the westerly side of the lake. The pier Flora is supposed to jump from points due west. All the camera would be able to see is a moving shadow and lens flare.

"Shit," I grumble, not for the first time that afternoon. I've said it each time I looked out the window, heard the thunder rumble, or caught a glimpse of lightning out of the corner of my eye. *Shit, shit, shit!* The weather was supposed to be agreeable this week. I can almost feel the production hemorrhaging money.

I reach for the walkie talkie on my cluttered dinette table and switch it to the appropriate frequency. "It's a wash," I announce without preamble. "We'll try again tomorrow. Get some sleep. MGM has comped rooms at the Lodge."

While the various units squawk their assent over the receiver, I prepare to head to the dingy hotel-cum-campsite myself. I could stay in my trailer amidst the detritus of my madness—a projector, various reels of telecined dailies, notebooks covered in manic scribbles, and various dog-eared copies of the script—but I need a change of scenery. I feel like a caged tiger, pacing back and forth, only able to catch glimpses of the grass he would rather be lazing in.

I pull on my poncho and step outside. It's only drizzling now, the clouds thick and gray. The thunder continues to resound, though it's softer now; the storm is moving toward the glacial valley of Yosemite to the east. A few crew members join me for the walk toward the Lodge, remarking about the weather, the shit luck of the production thus far, and whether that means we're "cursed."

I just grunt in response, dragging my shoulders up around my ears. I've never taken stock in curses before, but I've also never written a script while subsisting off whiskey and Obetrol. I've never created a monster from my own waking nightmare either. It's bad juju.

The Lodge consists of three separate sections: a squat log cabin, housing a gift shop and a bar; a two-story motel; and a large expanse where a guest can pitch a tent in a designated 2,500 square foot plot. Most of my cohorts head to the motel. I make a bee-line for the bar.

It's dark inside and reeks of cigar smoke. Native American tchotchkes decorate the walls, and a taxidermied black bear stands in the corner.

It's not crowded; only two men sit at the bar, their shoulders slumped as if the weight of the world is upon them. A bartender dries cups with a soiled rag, a hunk of chewing tobacco tucked into his pock-marked cheek.

I sit at the end of the bar and order a Rheingold beer, extra dry. The can is cool in my hand. "You're that director," the bartender says. It's a statement, not a question, and I wonder what gave me away.

"That's me," I say and take a swig of my beer. It's grainy with a smidge of fruitiness, but there is no hint of the inherent sweetness therein. It goes down as smoothly as water, the carbonation lingering on my tongue for only a moment.

"Shitty weather for filming, I imagine." The bartender pushes his long, wavy hair behind his ears with both hands, surveying me. His jaw clicks as he chews his tobacco, black goo speckling his dry lips.

I'm tired of talking about the *fucking* rain. "That's showbiz," I reply dryly. "Especially on location."

"What's yer movie about?"

Frankly, the movie is the last thing I'd like to discuss. But the man is eager for fresh conversation, and now that he's served me my drink, I'm obligated. Tit for tat.

I glance at the other two men at the bar. They look like two stalks planted in the same soil: slouch-backed, sun-weathered skin on their cheeks and noses, and with the far-off expressions of the overworked and underpaid. They are Lake Folk, the locals who shuttle tourists around in canoes or carry bags for a meager cash tip. Clearly, they aren't the talkative sort.

"It's a monster movie," I reply and take another slug of my beer.

"What sort of monster?" He rests his elbows on the bartop, interested.

"I guess you could say it's a werewolf of sorts." I hate that even saying the word aloud makes a shiver go down my spine. Surely, I can't summon them just by speaking the word aloud!

"Some of the guys out here really believe in that shit, did'ya know that? Me, though? I think they just got spooked by some big coyotes while smoking too much reefer." He pronounces "coyotes" with two syllables: ki-yotes.

An electric shock zings through my core. "Really?" Besides what I've read in books and experienced, I've found no evidence of wolf-men. It's been easy to discredit the books—some were fictional accounts, and others were written well before humans discovered critical thinking. I've started to doubt myself. Perhaps I mistook a ki-yote print for something more sinister too.

The bartender nods, gesturing toward one of the regulars. He's sitting at the other side of the bar, staring into his pint glass as if he can divine something from the dark amber liquid or the tufts of foam adorning the surface. "That's Robert Taneca. He actually owns the building you sittin' in right now. He was the one who told me 'bout seein' the werewolf."

"Do you think he'd talk to me? For research?"

"Buy him a drink. He'll talk yer ear off."

I slide off my stool, crushing the aluminum beer can in my hand. "Send over whatever he likes," I tell the bartender. "And another Rheingold too."

Robert Taneca doesn't acknowledge me as I sit upon the empty stool beside him. Instead, he pulls a leather cigarette case from his breast pocket and retrieves a lumpy, hand-rolled cigarette from inside. He lights it with a match then tosses the spent matchstick onto the mahogany bartop. He doesn't seem concerned that the lit match could burn the lacquered wood.

"I heard you saw a werewolf," I say, knowing no better way to strike up a conversation. Taneca doesn't seem the type to want to talk about bullshit.

He grunts, not looking at me. "I've seen a lot of things." He takes a drag of his cigarette before resting his bony wrist on the bartop.

The bartender appears with another pint and a can of Rheingold. "Compliments of your seatmate," he tells Taneca when the older man raises his bushy eyebrows.

"I was hoping you would tell me about it," I say once the bartender leaves us be. I pop the tab of my can, a wheezy, sustained *pshhh* of carbonation punctuating my words like an ellipsis.

"Why would a Hollywood prick want to hear about any of that?"

I try not to take the insult personally. I want to remind him that MGM booked his entire hotel for the week. He should be grateful; the Lodge is falling apart and clearly needs the money. The soap dish in my room fell off the wall just this morning, leaving a dark hole in which I could see pipes slick with condensation and dark water stains. But I suspect that won't get me anywhere.

"Because I think I encountered them out in Black Star Canyon," I reply, embarrassed by the not-quite-imperceptible stammer in my voice. "They surrounded my cabin."

It's the first time I've mentioned it aloud to anyone. Despite the overwhelming smell of cigarettes and stale sweat in the bar, I can smell the mothballs in the wardrobe again.

Taneca rests his elbow on the bartop, turning in his seat to look me in the eyes. His eyes are a rich hazel and remind me of sediment-heavy lake water, thick with minnows. I'd put my feet in Bass Lake earlier, and despite the ambient heat, the water was chilly. Taneca's gaze is chilly too—guarded. "Pal, if you truly experienced what you think you did, you would be dead."

"Well, I'm not. I know what I experienced. I heard them. They sounded human, and then they sounded like *wolves*." I whisper "wolves" as the bar's door opens, some members of the crew coming in for a drink. I tuck my chin into my shirt collar as if that will make me less recognizable. "I saw the tracks in the dirt the next day. They were enormous, bigger than a serving platter."

The crew members—three in total, Teamsters, I think—settle in at a nearby table. They don't seem to have noticed me. I relax my shoulders somewhat. "Please, Mr. Taneca," I murmur. "I've been doing some reading, but I'm not sure what is real. I'm … I think I'm losing it."

The older man takes a sip from his pint glass then wipes the excess off his upper lip with the back of his grizzled hand. "I have seen one," he relents.

He rises, reaching over the bar for a half-empty bottle of Jim Beam. "Come," he says, tucking the bottle beneath his thin jacket. "Let me show you."

♦ ♦ ♦

Robert Taneca lives in a small cabin a half-mile away from the Lodge's bar. We walk down the narrow, tree-lined path in silence, the only sound the crunch of gravel under our feet. He takes the bottle from his jacket after a quarter mile and unscrews the cap with a flourish. When he catches me staring, he raises his eyebrows. "Want some?" he asks, holding out the squarish bottle by its neck.

I shake my head. I'm walking into the woods with a stranger, after all; I need to have my wits about me. I find myself sizing him up as we walk side by side, trying to determine if I can overpower him if he's planning to cut off my skin and cook my innards. *Yes, I think I can.* He's much more slight than me, with only a hint of a bicep when he lifts the bottle to his lips. His belly hangs just over his belt buckle.

"What are you going to show me?" I ask when the lights of the Lodge have disappeared behind us. It's quite dark now, and I have to stare at the ground with my eyes screwed up to avoid tripping.

He says nothing until we reach the cabin. A dog barks inside until he shushes it with a "Shut your fucking mouth!" and a swift kick at the doorframe.

But instead of going inside, Taneca makes a beeline for a smaller building just beside the cabin. It's no more than an a-frame shack, a pile of cut wood just beneath its awning. "I'm going to show you the wolf," he says coolly, unlocking the heavy padlock on the flimsy door. I'm not entirely sure why he bothers to lock it. A determined person could break through the door with a little bit of momentum and a well-placed shoulder.

After opening the door, Taneca reaches up on tiptoes to pull the chain on a dangling lightbulb. It offers very little light and casts vague shadows that I realize are landscaping tools: a wheelbarrow, a rake and spade, a push mower, and various bags of fertilizer. It smells faintly of manure. Taneca grabs a flashlight off a shelf and turns it on with a flick of his calloused thumb. He points the beam into the deepest corner of the shack. "There he is. Go have a look."

I step around the man, curious. I inadvertently walk into the beam, and when I try to step aside, I collide with the rake, making it clatter to the ground. I yelp at the sudden sound, feeling foolish and emasculated. Taneca chuckles behind me. While I inch farther into the shack, Taneca adjusts the flashlight beam over my shoulder.

Then, I see it. Or rather, catch a glimpse of it. The beam bobs off and on the *creature's* face as if Taneca is having trouble steadying his hands. I want to wrench the flashlight out of his grip and use it myself. But I can't take my eyes off the creature laying on the dirt floor. When the beam pours into its eyes, it raises its hands—claws—to cover them, letting out a plaintive whine.

The creature is naked, its pinkish, wrinkly flesh streaked with dirt. It lays on its side, knees pulled up to its concave stomach. I can see the hollows of its ribs. A few cans of Red Heart dog food lay scattered around it, the lids mangled as if the can opener was too dull to do the job effectively.

During the flashlight beam's first pass over its body, I think it is a person, its ankle wrapped in a rusty chain. Adrenaline pours through me, but my limbs feel leaden. In fight, flight, or freeze, my body has chosen the latter. *Fuck*! I imagine Robert Taneca striking me over the head with the rake and tying me up just like the creature. Surely, he's a serial killer like H.H Holmes and what I'm looking at is a grotesque tableaux! But no attack comes.

On the second sweep of the flashlight's trembling beam, I see that the creature's face isn't humanoid, but canid. It's as though the person's head had been lobbed off with a very sharp blade, a wolf's sewn in its place. It looks bizarre, off-balance. I can't help but think of a phrase I found in my research: *caput gerat lupinum,* or "may he wear a wolfish head." It refers to a person who is deserving of death due to his heinous crimes. But what Robert Taneca has done here seems like a fate worse than death.

Curious, I step closer to the creature. I catch a brief glimpse of a swinging claw, a fur-covered shoulder, and the knots of its protruding spine before Taneca grabs the back of my shirt and hauls me out of the shed. Despite his old age, he's deceptively strong. He slams the door shut and puts the padlock back in place.

Inside the shed, I can hear the rattling of the chain and a whine. Then, the creature lets out a wailing howl. "What is that?" I pant.

"It's what you're looking for. Proof of it," Taneca replies coolly. "I shot it out in Yosemite. A silver bullet in the spine stopped it mid-transformation, paralyzed it from the chest down. Come into my cabin. We'll have a nightcap."

CHAPTER TEN
(DOMINIC)

◁◆▷

The monster makeup reeks of collodion, grease paint, and rubber. It makes me feel faintly heady, and I have to focus on my breathing to keep from swooning. When the application begins, I am immediately uncomfortable, desperate to step out of the chair for a cigarette and a bit of fresh air. But the collodion is flammable, and I'm too afraid that I'll set myself alight.

By the third hour of makeup application, being burned alive sounds preferable to my current circumstances. Ramón brings me coffee in a styrofoam cup, placing it into my hand. With the rubber narrowing my vision to a slit, I can't quite see the cup when I bring it to my mouth, and I dribble a bit down my collar.

After my face is finished, I am dressed in the rest of the costume. I wobble on the metal struts that give me an extra three feet of height and have to lean on Ramón's shoulder to walk to set. "MGM wants me to suffer," I lament.

Ramón chuckles, patting my back. "You brought this on yourself, pal."

"Some friend you are, Ramón del Olmo," I grumble.

"But I'm a good agent. You're getting paid extra for the days in costume."

"Pennies," I say with a snort.

We walk the short distance to the lakeside, finding the pier and the half-circle of cameras flanking it. Flora is standing on the dock with bare feet and a thin, ivory nightgown. She looks cold despite the summertime heat, rubbing at the gooseflesh on her arms. Her hair is styled like it was the night before—a rat's nest of twigs and leaves. I hate that the look is somewhat beguiling on her.

I was most attracted to Penelope after we were wolfish, our skin musky and our hair mussed. I would snare her wrist before she jumped into the shower, burying my nose into the curve of her neck and running the flat of my tongue over her skin. Many times, I bent her over the sink—her hands splayed like starfish on the mirror, her hot breath fogging the glass—desperate to feel her inner heat.

Otto Lang isn't on set. The assistant director, Paul *Something*, stands next to the camera, looking miffed. He's a young man, no older than I am, with a brushy mustache and a penchant for Madras sports coats. Today, he's wearing a red-and-green plaid one, which looks aggressively like Christmas in July. "Where's Lang?" I ask, my voice muffled by my rubber snout.

"He left a message. Said to shoot the sequence without him," Paul replies, adjusting the lapels on his coat. "My guess is he got a little too drunk at The Lodge. Some of the crew saw him there last night."

I scoff. If I had a hangover that kept me in bed, I would be lambasted. Otto would be outside of my trailer hammering on the doors and windows, threatening to call the studio. If I wasn't standing on struts, I would climb up the hill to the motel and do the same to him.

"We're going to start with the scene where Daphne is running from George, stopping just before the pier," Paul announces, raising his voice to be heard by all of the assembled crew. "Can we get the wig for Flora?" A random assistant appears with a hatbox, pulling out a wig that resembles Flora's hair—long and auburn, with a hint of a natural waviness. She affixes it over Flora's rat's nest.

"Alright, Dominic," Paul says. "How are you feeling on those stilts?"

"My legs are aching," I admit. I can already feel my joints gumming up, unaccustomed to the strange foot position and uneven terrain. My left knee sears, grinding in its socket whenever I shift my weight.

"We are going to have you chase Flora from *there,*" he gestures to a tree a few yards away, "to the dock. Do you think you can handle a run?"

"We can always speed it up in post, right?" I joke, but he's clearly not receptive to it. His lip doesn't even twitch. "I can do it," I mumble, feeling rejected.

"Good. We'll try to get it in one or two takes." He steps away to briefly talk to the camera crew then calls Flora and me to our marks. Flora ignores me, her eyes glued on the assistant director as he gives us final instructions. I'm not listening. Instead, I survey Flora through my mask's obstructed eye holes.

I wonder what she looks like wolfish. Is her fur red like her hair? Is she long-limbed with a tapered waist like a greyhound or taut with corded muscle like a mastiff?

I meant what I said. This town will annihilate her. It's already taking its toll. She's been biting her nails, the ragged edges filled with acrylic Nu Nails and covered with a glossy topcoat. She's lost weight too, her clavicle jutting out like the crisscross posts at a railroad crossing. *Danger, danger.* But despite the apparent stress, she was defiant and laughed in my face. *Pardon me for not prostrating myself before you.* It made my skin burn as though she put her hands on me.

Paul steps away to slump into the director's chair, his knees spread wide. "Cameras ready?" he asks the three camera operators spread in an arc to get the perfect angle.

"Ready," they say, nearly in unison.

"Quiet on set," Paul says, raising his voice for everyone to hear. "Roll sound."

"Sound speeding," pipes up the man with the boom mic hovering over my head.

The assistant with the clapboard appears beside me. "Scene fifty-two, take one," he mumbles around his cigar, the acrid smoke tricking through the gaps in my mask. I feel as though I might sneeze, which I'm sure will cause some of the prosthetics to fly off my face. I screw up my nose until the feeling abates.

"Set," chirps the lead camera operator, fiddling with the various knobs and buttons on the side of the camera.

"And *action*," Paul finishes, leaning forward in his chair.

Flora breaks into a run, and I catch the tiniest crinkle of a smile at the corner of her lips when she turns away from the camera. I give chase, the struts encasing my lower legs squeaking. My gait is undignified—a lurching lollop more than a run. I want to stop and complain, but it will only prolong my time in the costume. A trickle of sweat—or is it greasepaint?—edges down my neck and under the thick, knobby rubber of the breastplate.

I let out a roar, and Flora shrieks in response. She trips in the grass but regains her footing, her toes curling in the dirt. She looks over her shoulder at me, and for a moment, I see genuine terror there. Her red-rimmed eyes bulge.

Suddenly, she trips again, tumbling into the grass. The sole of her foot collides with my strut, and I wobble, nearly toppling onto her. I let out a roar, waiting for her to get up and continue on. Paul hasn't said "Cut" yet, and I'll be damned if I have to do this miserable scene again.

Flora looks up at me, her hazel eyes brimming with tears. Except, there's something odd about her face—an angularness in her jaw as though it has come unhinged in the fall. Her lips part, and I see the needle points of her incisors, the wicked edge of an overly large canine. *Shit!*

Without thinking, I squat down, clapping my enormous hands over her face. I feel the bones of her skull shifting beneath the rubbery paw pads, and I spread my fingers so I can see her right eye. Her pupils are dilated, black voids that reflect my own gruesome facade. "Flora," I hiss, unsure if she can even hear me through the layers of rubber, collodion, and greasepaint. "You need to control yourself."

Her teeth chatter. "I can't. I don't know what's happening." Her voice is an octave too high, the consonants seeming to get stuck in her throat as though she's seen a g-g-ghost!

Over my shoulder, several yards away, Paul shouts, "Cut, cut! What the *fuck* is going on?" I only have a few seconds. No one can see her like this.

"Flora, close your eyes," I murmur, trying to make my voice kind. I'm not terribly convincing, but she's thrashing for a proverbial life raft. Even a jagged rock pocked with barnacles looks like salvation in the churning waves.

After a second of hesitation, she does as I ask, her eyelid crinkling like crepe paper. Her brow tightens. "Breathe," I urge. "Focus on my voice. This wasn't real—you're safe."

I can hear Paul's footsteps. He'll be here in a moment. "That's it," I tell her as her breathing slows. The wolfish snout against my palm recedes. I stroke her jawline with my thumbs, knowing bones knitting back together is painful.

Slowly, I take my hands away, finding her face flushed but human. *Thank you*, she mouths just before Paul reaches us. The assistant director looks worse than Flora does; he's sweating profusely, his face beet red. "What happened?" he asks. "Are you alright?"

"I tripped," Flora says, sitting up. "The air was knocked out of me. I'm alright." Her voice wobbles, and she wipes away an errant tear with her knuckle. "I'm sorry."

"Do you think you can try again? After we get you in a clean dress?"

Despite the persisting tremble in her lip, Flora nods. Streaked with dirt and damp from last night's rain, the fall has made her look not unlike a swamp creature herself. Pieces of grass stick to her skin, dirt caps her quickly bruising elbow, and her wig has been knocked askew. As if summoned, Flora's makeup artist appears with a thick towel, wrapping it around her shoulders.

"Let's take twenty," Paul says, projecting his voice so the assembled crew can hear.

We shoot the scene without incident after the break and several more angles besides. Afterward, I linger in video village, watching Flora shoot her scene in the water. Ramón asks if I want to go back to my trailer, but I wave him away, my eyes on the actress.

In this sequence, she's fallen off the dock in an attempt to escape the monster, and she bursts from beneath the water with a gasp. It's a mere five seconds of film, but Paul is looking for perfection. Each time she emerges from beneath the murky lake water, gasping and flailing, he shakes his head. "I don't believe you're frightened; you look like you're having a spa day. Push your hair back before you gasp, the audience is paying to see your face. Push the gown off your shoulder. You look too put together."

She just nods, waiting for the cue to dunk herself again. Whatever shook her confidence this morning is gone now; she is game for whatever the assistant director asks her to do. It makes me curious. *What happened earlier?* Surely, it wasn't my costume.

I peel off my mask, the baking Californian air feeling surprisingly cool on my overheated skin. Sitting in the canvas chair is awkward, my stilts far too long to bend properly. An exasperated Teamster has to high-step over them, his arms laden with film canisters and a loop of extension cord. I don't move out of the way. I am certain that if I watch long enough, I will parse the mystery of Flora's near-breakdown.

I also find myself wanting to catch a glimpse of her in the waterlogged dress, the semi-transparent fabric clinging to her every curve. Surely, some of the shots won't get past the Hays Code's stringent nudity clause.

"Otto's back," Ramón murmurs, jabbing my shoulder.

I look up to see the director striding toward set, a cup of coffee in hand. He is wearing the same clothes he was the day before, the mustard stain on his breast pocket in the shape of Arkansas. His greasy hair lays flat upon his forehead, and his cheek is sleep-creased as though he just rolled out of bed. I recognize the look of the woefully hungover. His face is pale, and his lips blanched as though he might vomit at any moment.

"He looks like shit," Ramón observes. "Worse than you do after a night at the Chateau."

Otto offers me a brief nod before continuing toward the dock. Paul looks disappointed to see him, clearly enjoying his time in the driver's seat. "I think we got the shots," he tells his boss, his tone guarded.

"Get the film developed, and we will watch the dailies this evening," Otto grumbles. "*Then*, I'll decide if we got the shots."

CHAPTER ELEVEN
(FLORA)

───────◁◆▷───────

I hold the phone receiver against my ear, listening to the plaintive *riii-iiiing* over the line. "Pick up," I murmur, desperate to hear Ama's voice. I expect it will be a comfort, like wrapping oneself in an enormous woolen blanket.

It rings six times before she finally picks up, and I nearly burst into tears when I hear her sing-song, "Hello?"

"Thank God! I thought you weren't home," I exclaim.

"Flora! How is the Golden State treating you?" I hear rustling and imagine Ama draping herself upon her overstuffed couch, tangling her fingers in the curlicue phone cord. She can't help but fiddle with it, needing something to do with her hands. I can picture her so clearly in my mind's eye, and I burst into tears. She patiently listens to me bawl until the sobs turn into sniffles. "Tell me what's going on," she prompts, her voice gentle.

"I nearly turned wolfish on set today," I manage. "That's never happened to me before."

Her gasp floats over the phone line. "Did anyone see?"

"No, well, *yes*. Dominic did." I briefly catch her up on the happenings with Dominic Valentine over the last several weeks: his volatile attitude when we met, the evening before when he accosted me in my trailer, and finally, the way he held me in his hands on the lakeside.

I can still feel the rubber of his gloves, the tickle of the faux fur between his fingers. There was a curious smell to his costume—unnaturally sweet, so much so it read as toxicity. It made me faintly heady. Or had my own impending transformation made me feel punch drunk? Even with the mask, I could see just a hint of his eye, the iris a rich ocher like a cup of steeping coffee. His voice was soft and as gentle as the waves that lapped against my feet on the beach in Wharton. I'd never heard him use that voice before. I'd only heard him grumble, growl, or grouse.

"Why did it happen?" Ama asks. In the background, I hear their sliding glass door roll open and the excited shriek of her four-year-old daughter, Olivia. Rafe's warm baritone follows, but I can't quite make out the words. "Sorry," Ama apologizes as the voices recede and a door closes, "they just got back from the beach."

My heart aches. I miss going to the beach with my de facto niece. Olivia loved to dig in the sand, searching for sand fleas to play with. The minuscule crabs would be subjected to mazes she'd designed—labyrinthine corridors scooped out with a plastic shovel. Most of the crabs would simply dig their own escape tunnels before reaching the end, not understanding their pre-scribed mission.

"It's going to sound silly," I warn her.

"Try me."

"I was running from Dominic, who was dressed as the monster. It's a silly costume, especially up close. You can see bits of Dom's skin at the seams, and his breath was far too loud. He was huffing and puffing like he had run a marathon. But if I laughed, it would have ruined it. So I tried really hard to think of some-thing frightening, and I did." I whisper the last two words as though they are a secret.

Ama makes an encouraging noise. *Go on*, she says without saying anything at all.

"So then I found myself thinking about Elton." It's strange to say the name of my former friend aloud. I've avoided it as though those two syllables were imbued with dark power. *El-ton:* a curse, an anathema, an invi-tation for the evil eye to look upon me.

"Oh," Ama murmurs. I wait for her to tell me to stop, but she doesn't. I wouldn't blame her if she did.

"We were friends, you know," I babble, not wanting to let the line go quiet. If I do, I won't be able to find my voice again; the silence will be far too oppressive, too thick to wade through. "I watched his children a lot so that he and Mags could get some time away. The girls called me 'auntie'. When I found out what he had done to Rafe, to you, to Nico, I—" I swallow a lump of emotion in my throat. "I tried so hard to picture it. I was torturing myself. Truly. I would lay awake at night, running through what little I knew, filling in the gaps. It was the only way I could wrap my mind around it, y'know?"

Ama makes a soft noise somewhere between a sigh and a murmur.

"I never asked what he was like that night. But I think I have a good idea. Elton was always so quick to anger. Once, he clenched his fists so hard that his knuckles turned white like bone. You should have seen the look in his eyes—they were empty, as though painted on. I thought he was going to swing at Mags' head just because she dared ask where he was for hours on end." While I talk, I toy with the tassels on the throw blanket draped over my lap, worrying the threads between my fingers until they unravel.

"So, when Dominic was chasing me, I pictured Elton's face," I continue. "Then, when I tripped, my body reacted before I could remind myself it wasn't real, that someone would eventually yell 'cut.'"

"It sounds like Dominic protected you and your secret," Ama says, always one to look for the bit of sunlight peeking through the storm clouds.

He did.

"That's what I can't figure out. *Why?*"

"Well, he's an Alpha, isn't he? That's what Alpha wolves do," Ama replies, matter-of-factly.

I can't help but chuckle. Ama is thinking, of course, of her husband. Rafe is the quintessential Alpha—strong, chivalrous, selfless. Dominic is none of those things. He's selfish, testy, and can even be cruel. If he is truly the Alpha here, he strong-armed his way up the ladder, baring his teeth at whomever stood between him and the throne.

"I can't help but think he has ulterior motives," I muse. "I don't think something like that is beneath him at all."

CHAPTER TWELVE
(OTTO)

———◁◆▷———

The projector makes a *clack-clack-clack* sound as the reel abruptly unspools, the tape flailing like a banner of surrender. I stare at the square of white light on the trailer wall, chewing at my nails. *Clack-clack-clack!* "Play it again."

"Sure thing, boss." Paul gets up from his spot on the couch, setting aside his citron bottle of 7-Up. I faintly hear the beverage fizzing. He rethreads the film with nimble fingers, humming a discordant tune to himself.

"I want to see the first take again."

"Really? That one is useless." Paul reloads the film canister nonetheless, and a frozen image appears on-screen. It's a close-up of Flora's face, half-obscured by what I imagine is her blurry arm flung above her head. She's mid-fall, seconds from landing upon the damp earth.

"Don't bother rewinding. Start there," I insist. Paul flips the switch to start the film then settles back onto the couch.

On screen, Flora flops like an oxygen-deprived salmon, her mouth agape. The fall forcibly ejected the air from her lungs, and it takes her several gulps to fill them again. Slowly, she props herself up onto her elbows. From this angle, I can see her face in profile: her bulging right eye, weeping tears; her jaw ratcheting tight to tamp down the encroaching sobs; and the pulsating temporal artery near her hairline, keeping time with the staccato of her heartbeat.

I've seen many women cry on set. Hell, I've made them cry if it suits my vision. But they don't ever look like Flora does. There's immeasurable pain there, as though she's broken a bone in her fall. "Was Flora hurt?" I ask as Dominic moves into the frame, kneeling over her.

"No. There was a little scrape on her elbow, but the makeup artist covered it before the next take."

Dominic's gloved hands hover over Flora as if unsure whether to pick her up or leave her in the damp grass. Suddenly, he claps both hands over her face. "Can you rewind a few seconds?" I ask.

Paul gets up to do as I ask, though he certainly doesn't move as quickly as he did earlier. He clearly thinks this is pointless or, worse, a *lesson*. I expect he's waiting for me to jab at the projected image and shout something like "*That's* your mistake right there, Paul!" My assistant director threads the film back by a handful of frames then turns it back on.

There!

It's brief, but just before Dominic's hands obscure Flora's face, her jaw seems to shoot forward like a goblin shark's. I catch a glimpse of a row of teeth, decidedly carnivorous in nature. "Did you see that?" I ask Paul, leaning forward in my seat.

"See what?" he asks, still standing beside the projector.

"Again," I nearly shout. "Show me again."

Paul sighs but carefully adjusts the fragile film strip in its reel. Again, I watch Flora's jaw contort and Dominic clap his hands over the horrific scene. "Did you see it?" I ask again.

Paul shrugs. "I don't see anything. Maybe a bit of warping. Perhaps some of the acetate in the film reel decayed before we used it."

"That's unlikely," I say with a scoff. "There aren't any other artifacts. Don't you see her *face*?"

Paul shakes his head, raising his eyebrows at me. "It's just her face. It looks like the fall hurt. Are you okay, boss?" He glances pointedly at his sporty Submariner watch. "It's getting late. Maybe you need to get some rest and look at this in the morning." Without waiting for a response, he turns the projector off, the already dark room becoming an inky black.

"You can go," I say dismissively, waving him away. Paul doesn't argue with me. Instead, he picks up his 7-Up and gives me a little salute with it. A few drops slosh onto the floor.

"Get some sleep, Otto," he says seriously. "You look like hell."

I watch the two seconds of footage over and over, oscillating wildly between thinking it's genuine and a film defect. It's as though my brain can't bear to accept it even though I've seen it with my own two eyes.

When my eyelids grow heavy around midnight, I cut thick lines of powdered Benzedrine with my Diners' Club card and snort them off my dinette table. Sleep is dangerous. Sleep is the equivalent of slathering my body with Worcestershire sauce and ketchup. *Come have a taste!*

Robert Taneca tosses a log into the fireplace, and the sudden shower of sparks makes me jump. I sit facing the cabin's picture window, convinced that, at any moment, the wolf-creature will escape its bindings and come looking for retribution. I imagine it tearing the flimsy shed apart, throwing aside its chains as though as inconsequential as a skein of yarn. From my seat, I can just make out the sagging roof of the shed, a kitschy rooster weathervane adorning its highest point. If I listen very carefully, I can hear the weathervane squeaking as the breeze rotates it.

Taneca's squat basset hound sniffs at my muddy shoes. Without looking at the animal, I stroke his silky head, scratching behind his heavy ears with my index fingers. His fur makes my hands feel greasy. "How long has it been out there?" I ask. Saying "it" feels absurd, but I'm not sure how else to refer to the monster. Surely, it's not a person.

Taneca lounges on his threadbare couch, his feet propped upon the Depression-era coffee table. The older man is far more relaxed than I am, his back to the window.

He took his shoes off just inside the front door, and it is apparent that his underwear is just as homespun as his outerwear. There's a hole in his sock, his big toe sticking out. The nail is thick and stinks like rancid cheese—a fungal infection, I think. "A few months," he grunt. "I caught it sniffing around when I was hunting turkey."

"The books ...they never said it would look like that." I shudder at the memory of the half-wolf chimera, its body horrifically warped. I can't stop thinking about its ostensibly human eyes, set deeply in the wolf's eye sockets. They were wet with unshed tears, the moisture catching the meager light of the flashlight. It made it look as though its eyes were twinkling.

"I shot it with my Remington, and the bullet is lodged in its spine. It's paralyzed. I don't think it can choose its form now." No wonder he's so composed; the beast has no means of escape.

"Why did you keep it?" The hound, tiring of my attention, wanders off to flop on its belly beside the hearth, heaving a deep, human-like sigh. Its loose skin pools around it.

Taneca reaches for a small box on the coffee table and opens it to reveal a few cigars, a double-bladed cigar cutter, and a lighter. "Do you want one?" he asks as he rolls a cigar between his calloused fingers. I shake my head. He cuts off the tip then lights it, careful to make sure it is burning evenly. When he takes a drag, bluish smoke pours out of his nostrils. "I keep it as a warning to the others," he finally answers.

"The others?" I gulp.

"They are like cockroaches. There's always more." He says it casually, as though we are talking about any invasive pest like rabbits in the garden or bats in the attic.

I pick at a loose thread on the chair's armrest. "I still can't believe they're real," I murmur to myself more than to him. It's as though I stumbled through a portal into another world during my nighttime stroll in Black Star Canyon. Or perhaps I fell into a crevasse and am now wedged tight between two boulders, hallucinating!

"You people never do—cityfolk, I mean. You don't see somethin' unless it's right in front of your face," Taneca grumbles. "But out here, it's different."

Suddenly, I hear a plaintive howl from the shed. It's a reedy, strangled sound, as heartbreaking as the dulcet tones of Tony Bennett's "Blue Velvet." The song always made me tearful, reminding me of fires long extinguished and relationships that have run their course. A chill edges down my spine, and despite the warm fire, gooseflesh prickles on my arms. I feel strangely sad for the creature.

"He's crying for his pack," Taneca says matter-of-factly, ashing his cigar in a puke-green glass ashtray. "But they won't come for him. They haven't yet, anyway."

"It sounds so sad." I still can't bear to refer to it as "he" or "him", though Taneca does so with ease. Perhaps I don't want to humanize it, knowing it's imprisoned. No person should have to live like that—naked, chained, licking dog food out of sharp-edged cans, and slurping rainwater out of the cracks in the wall.

"Don't let it fool you," Taneca warns, jabbing the burning end of his cigar in my direction. "It'll eat you if you give it an inch. Any of 'em will. They aren't like us even though, sometimes, they got human faces."

To prove his point, he rolls up his shirtsleeve to his elbow, showing me a half-moon of atrophic imprints in his skin, the deeper ones keloidal. It looks like he was punctured by dozens of miniature ice picks. "The bastard tried to rip my arm off. He pretended to be a tourist, said he got bit by a snake and needed help. When I came over with the first aid kit," Taneca slams his fist upon the chair's wooden armrest, the bang *making me jump, "he attacked me."*

"What causes it? The books I've been reading all say different things: a magical salve, a bite or scratch, rabies, a punishment from a scorned god, enchanted clothes..."

Taneca shrugs. "Does it matter?"

I think of the night in my wardrobe, cowering, bladder bursting. Yes, it does matter.

Maybe it's a malformation in their genetic make-up—a syndrome," Taneca muses. "Y'know, like a foal born with one eye in the center of its forehead or a lamb with two heads. 'Cept, this one's sneaky. You can't catch it at birth, when it's easy to snap its neck."

The creature howls again, and I feel as though I'm coming unglued. My joints feel loose, and my insides are watery. I can't bear to hear the sound again. I want to go back to my hotel room and hide under the fetid bedsheets made rank by my night sweats. I want to drink from the bottle of Old Crow I keep in the mini fridge until my eyes grow heavy, sucking on it like a baby bottle. Surely, tomorrow, I can pretend this never happened at all. Oh, what did I do last night? I drank at The Lodge and went back to my room, thank you for asking.

I lurch to my feet. "I've got to go," I manage. "It's late."

The old man simply surveys me, not bothering to rise. His cigar is just a nub now, and he jabs it against the bottom of the ashtray. The movement splits the wrapper, filling the small room with the acrid smell of spent tobacco. He adjusts himself in the chair, resting his right ankle on his left knee and his bristly chin on his palm.

"You said you saw them near your home," he murmurs. "That means they know what you smell like now."

I skirt around the coffee table and step over the dozing dog. "I have to get back," I babble. "There's an early call in the morning and—"

"Shoot them first," Taneca continues, unruffled by my hasty move toward the exit. "Right between the fucking eyes. If you wait, it'll be too late."

The wolf howls again just as I pull open the door. The balmy air wraps me up in a hug, and for a moment, it is difficult to breathe. As I pick my way down the path, blind in the pitch dark, I have to walk very close to the shed. The creature whines. "Help," it says with a glottal fry. "Help me."

"I can't," I whisper, not thinking it can hear me over the rattling of its chains or through the wall between us.

"I hope they hunt you, then," it cries. "I hope they hunt you."

CHAPTER THIRTEEN
(DOMINIC)

◁◆▷

I've missed you, Los Angeles.

I lean back against the leather couch, letting my eyes ease closed. Dimly, I am aware of a tug at my zipper, and I lift my hips, letting Penelope pull my slacks down to my upper thigh. Her breath is hot against my underwear, and I twine my fingers in her hair, urging her onward. "Don't be a tease," I cajole. "You know how much I've missed you."

She hums in response, her fingers hooking the waistband of my y-fronts, easing them down. The sharp edges of her nails against my sensitive flesh make me shiver in anticipation. Trysts with Penelope are like bread and butter—classic, with the decadence that is lost with lesser spreads.

Flora is surely margarine.

Before I can delve into why I'm thinking about Flora, Penelope's glossy lips encircle my cock. Her tongue slathers over my head, and I grip her scalp, guiding her ministrations with gentle pressure. Penny is not one to shrivel up at a challenge, and she takes me completely into her mouth, my bulbous head edging just past her soft palate. Her hands tightly grip my thighs, digging her nails in just enough to leave red half-moons behind. "Good girl," I croon.

Someone knocks on my trailer door. *Fuck!* Penelope sits back on her heels, wiping at her slick mouth with the back of her hand. "It's Ramón," she whispers, gesturing at the Ramón-shaped shadow behind the frosted glass.

"He can wait," I grumble. My cock stands stiffly between us, aching for her touch.

Penelope looks up at me with serious, cyan eyes, her lips downturned. "Are you shooting a scene today?"

"In an hour," I fib, knowing I have to be on set in ten minutes. I'm dreading it. Today, we're shooting a romantic scene between Daphne and George, and I don't particularly want to kiss Flora. What I *want* is for Penelope to make me feel so good I forget about it entirely. "I'll be out in a minute!" I shout to Ramón. His shadow shifts from foot to foot.

"Is Penny here?" he calls. "Some of the crew have mentioned seeing her."

Shit. I thought I had been so clandestine, sneaking Penelope onto the backlot and into my trailer. But her face—and the signature beauty mark upon her high forehead—is as recognizable as Marilyn Monroe's. I was a fool to think no one would pay her any mind, especially with her arm linked around *my* waist. "No," I lie.

Penny snickers, rising from between my legs and straightening her skirt. I shoot her a pained look, but she pays me no mind, and I stuff myself—still achingly hard—back into my slacks.

"Hello, Penelope," Ramón says dryly as she opens the door. He quickly secures the door before prying eyes catch sight of my visitor. "You *had* to pull this stunt today, didn't you?" he grumbles, addressing me now. "Otto is in a foul mood. The journalist from *Daily Variety* is here to interview the cast, and all *anyone* is talking about is Penelope Cox being on set. This is going to end up in the fucking magazine."

Penelope steps into the trailer's cubicle bathroom and checks her lipstick in the mirror. She left the door ajar, and from the sofa, I can see the luscious curve of her hip. My cock spasms in my pants. I wish I had the time to undress her, to sink my teeth into her thick haunch until my mouth filled with her thick fur. *God*.

Ramón interprets my silence as surliness; he isn't entirely wrong. "There's only a week left of filming. One fucking week. Couldn't you have behaved for a few more days?"

"I'm so sorry, Ramy," Penelope calls from the bathroom. "If I had known a reporter was here, I wouldn't have come." Finally, she emerges and sits beside me on the sofa. "I can sneak out."

"Thank you," Ramón exclaims. "At least *one* of you has sense."

✦ ✦ ✦

The crew on Studio H's bedroom set is bare-bones—a skeleton crew. It's common when shooting a romantic scene, to keep everyone's dignity intact. It seems like overkill for this scene. It's much more tame than what happened in my trailer moments before. Daphne and George simply kiss then tumble together, fully clothed, onto the bedspread. It's a suggestion of what is to come, not so much an illustration of what is happening.

Typically, I like shooting these scenes. After all, more often than not, I'm already sleeping with my costar. These scenes serve as a flirtation, often culminating in wild sex in a private trailer afterward. But Flora isn't my girlfriend, she's the thorn in my side.

Flora Wright, always on time, perches on the edge of the large, four-poster bed. She's wearing a circle dress, the polka-dot skirt pooling atop the bedspread. Her auburn hair is loose and draped over her shoulder. She fiddles with the ends, tangling it around her fingers. If she isn't careful, it will become irreparably knotted and need to be cut. She's nervous.

Before I can step up onto the sound stage, a man steps into my path. He's clearly a reporter, as evident by his pad of paper and open-mouthed countenance. It's as though he is waiting to gulp down gossip like sustenance, akin to a goldfish waiting for its owner to pour papery flakes into its fishbowl. "Stan Chesterfield, *Daily Variety*," he chirps, bouncing on his toes. "How are you doing, Dominic?"

He's not really asking how I'm doing. It's a fake out meant to make me feel congenial and off-guard.

Stan Chesterfield, *Daily Variety*, wants me to think we are friends, pals, bosom buddies. "I'm late," I reply.

"We can walk and talk," he counters smoothly, matching my pace and following me onto the stage. He's like a mosquito. How I wish I could slap him away! "The rumor mill is abuzz," he continues, "about you and Flora Wright. But we're also hearing that Penelope Cox is on set today. Can you clear that up?"

At the mention of Penelope's name, Flora's head snaps around. I can almost hear her cervical spine crack in her haste. Her eyes are as round as saucers. "Penelope Cox is *here*?" Her startled reaction plays into the reporter's narrative, and he scribbles something on his pad. I groan inwardly.

A sudden grating noise in the rafters draws our attention, and distracted, we look up. Otto Lang stomps across the metal catwalk above our heads, bits of dirt clinging to the soles of his boots falling through the diamond-shaped grating like a gentle, springtime rain. As he heads down the stairs, his hand tailing upon the rail, I notice that he looks even worse than he did at Bass Lake. There's a new patch of scaly eczema on his cheek, and he keeps sniffling as though he has a lingering cold.

"Let's get this show on the road," Otto announces, coughing dryly into his fist. His voice sounds hoarse and gritty, as though he swallowed a fistful of crushed glass. "Marks!" He doesn't even offer us a glance, merely slumping in his director's chair.

Stan Chesterfield clears his throat. "Mr. Lang, Stan Chesterfield from *Daily Varie—*"

"Quiet on the set," Otto interrupts, clapping his hands together. In the cavernous studio space, the sound reverberates off the rafters until it reads as sustained applause. He's still not looking at us, his bloodshot eyes on the cement floor and his own twitching feet.

Stan's eyebrows rise to meet his hairline. "Is he alright?" he asks with a sidelong look in my direction, jerking a thumb at the director. Slumped in his chair, it appears as though Otto has fallen asleep save for the click of his jaw as he chews the air.

Otto has always been a strange man; he is, after all, an artist. Artists are characteristically peculiar, their heads in the clouds and their legs half-mired in the muck of uncertainty. It's a split existence: longing for preeminence but knowing that a misplaced curb will shatter their teeth. After all, what is art but creating wings that could melt if they are spread too close to the sun? On the first day we met, it was clear that Otto was no exception to this. He addressed me with his back ramrod straight and his knuckles clenched, but he winced as he spoke as if expecting me to whack his snout with a rolled-up newspaper.

Since Bass Lake, he has been different. He spent the last two days there pawning scenes off on Paul but would stand in the back of video village with his arms crossed. He stopped addressing the cast directly, the assistant director his mouthpiece. Most of what Paul said started with "Otto wants..."

Otto's nose streamed with snot, his sinuses inflamed by whatever drug he's been snorting. He started wearing sunglasses, presumably because the sunlight hurt his perpetually dilated pupils. Once, I passed him on the way to my trailer, and he grabbed my arm, babbling, "Did you see it too?" I told him I didn't know what he was talking about, and he sighed so hard he seemed to deflate. "Of course, of course. It was just in my head."

But I don't tell Stan Chesterfield this. It's time to circle the wagons. As much as I despise Otto Lang and this film, I won't align myself with a *journalist*. "We've all been working hard," I reply—a non-answer. "You heard the man: 'Quiet on set.'"

CHAPTER FOURTEEN
(FLORA)

———◁◆▷———

I'm so edgy it feels as though ants are crawling beneath my skin. Knowing that the actress I most admire is on set makes the sensation unbearable. I find myself scanning video village, looking for her signature sand-colored hair and willowy figure. Not finding her there is a relief.

I'm fairly certain that I will vomit all over the bodice of my dress if one more accelerant is added to the proverbial pile of kindling. Ingrid had stacked the wood herself this morning, shadowing me as I traversed the lot between the hair and makeup trailers.

"There are certain rules for scenes like this," Ingrid had said. "If you break them, you'll waste the director's time and tarnish your reputation."

Scenes like this: romantic encounters, stolen kisses, implied lovemaking.

"What do you mean?" I asked as I settled into a chair. Without preamble, the makeup artist pats beige

powder onto my cheeks and forehead, murmuring under her breath about a reddish blemish at my hairline. The synthetic wig used at Bass Lake had irritated my skin, leaving itchy, scaly patches behind.

"The Hays Code keeps everyone modest, and it makes Hollywood more appealing to the common, decent man. It's your job to toe the line between modesty and titillation. We want the viewer to feel something, but not anything untoward."

To me, that seems like a strange tightrope to walk. Daphne and George are a married couple; surely, there's nothing immoral about showing that they love one another. "What are the rules?" *I ask.*

While she speaks, Ingrid ticks off points on her well-manicured fingers. "In a love scene, you can only kiss without lust for three seconds; you can't be shown sharing a bed unless you have one foot on the floor throughout the scene; no nudity, either implied or in actuality; and there's absolutely no sexual simulation."

"Goodness," *I remark, closing my eyes so that the makeup artist can apply eyeshadow up to my brow bone.*

"According to the Code, scenes in the bedroom must have 'good taste and delicacy'." *Ingrid chuckles.* "What they really want is for the scene to be boring. We can't have moviegoers in the flyover states thinking we are a hotbed of moral corruption, can we?"

I swallow a hard lump that has suddenly settled into my esophagus. "What happens if we break the rules?"

"Either Otto has to recut the film to get approval, or it gets canned entirely. Then, all that work Carver

Merlotte put into you is a waste. You certainly won't be offered another opportunity."

On set, the *Daily Variety* reporter finally steps off the sound stage, propelled by whatever Dominic said to him. I haven't been listening, too distracted by the intrusive thoughts tumbling through my skull. This scene—kissing Dominic Valentine—has been a cliff edge on the horizon, and now, suddenly, I'm wavering with my toes over the edge.

"Marks!" Otto repeats, exasperated. I haven't moved to my bit of duct tape, dead center in the middle of the bedroom set. Dominic steps casually onto his own mark, his hands in his pockets. Moving much more slowly, I join him, the studio lights instantly making me sweat.

"Action," Otto calls.

Dominic's fingers alight on my arms, barely touching my skin. Gooseflesh prickles there, making the thin hairs on my forearms stand on end. "Daphne," he croons, "you stayed. Despite everything, you stayed."

As always, it is disquieting to watch George's husbandly façade slip over Dominic's hard exterior. He may as well have put on a mask made of rubber. Even his eyes change—cold, hard obsidian softening to warm, liquid cocoa. It makes my blood hot, turning my cheeks a lively pink.

Can he see it, even with the stage lights in his eyes?

"I love you, George. All of you. Even..." I reach up to stroke his cheek with my palm, following the script's action sequence to the letter. Inadvertently, the pad of my thumb brushes against the petal-soft corner of his lip. His hot breath wets my skin. "Even if you frighten me," I finish, all too aware of the slight wobble in my voice.

This close, I can't help but smell the wolfishness on his skin—musky and woodsy. I can't believe I once mistook it for cologne. How could such a complex fragrance possibly be bottled? Surely, it couldn't be manufactured by human hands.

Dominic pulls me close, dipping his chin so that our mouths are inches apart. Our breath commingles, mine fast and his even. I am only somewhat cognizant of the camera as it noisily edges forward on its track, keen on getting a close-up shot of our faces in profile.

Abruptly, Dominic's mouth connects with mine. The kiss is chaste, as light as a feather. I find myself counting.

One Mississippi.

Dominic's hand cups my cheek, his thumb sliding down the slope of my jawline. Molten heat pours between my legs, and I hate that my body can't differentiate between playacting and reality. *This isn't real!* I scream, inwardly. Surely, I don't want it to be real. Do I?

Two Mississippi.

Dominic walks me back until my calves collide with the bed. He turns me away from the camera's prying eye for a moment, and, surreptitiously, he slips his tongue into my mouth. He tastes faintly of wintergreen toothpaste. *That* wasn't in the script. I feel faintly heady, and my fingers tangle in the fabric of his shirt-front to keep from swooning.

Three Mississippi.

Dominic breaks the kiss and guides me backward onto the bed. The mattress is firm, and the blankets smell faintly of sawdust and the detritus of stagecraft. I anticipate the weight of his body atop mine and find myself longing for it despite the burning in my face.

Just as Dominic places a knee onto the bed, Otto yells, "Cut!" As if released from a spell—or rather, a curse—Dominic blinks, looking down at me as if I'm a stranger. Then, his patented sneer overtakes his face, turning him ugly. I expect a snide remark, but then Otto is onstage, gesticulating animatedly. "That was a great take 'til you fucked it up, Dom. You know your angles."

"I misstepped." Dominic shrugs.

"Let's go again," Otto grumbles. "We need five minutes to reset."

I sit up in bed, waiting for him to give me feedback too, but he doesn't acknowledge me at all. In fact, he pointedly avoids my gaze, his stance ramrod straight as though under inspection. I wonder if it is because the reporter is lingering. Stan Chesterfield from *Daily Variety* is still standing near the stage, scribbling on his pad with a nub of a pencil.

Did he notice Dominic's teasing kiss? It had to have been meant to humiliate me. Dominic wanted to rattle me, to remind me that I don't belong here. *You are out of your element, Flora Wright!* he'd said with a slither of his tongue.

As set dressers come to fluff the pillows and smooth the sheets and Otto turns to address the cameraman, Dominic hops offstage, making a beeline for the craft services table. I follow him, incensed. "What was that?" I growl.

"What was what?" he asks as he casually fills a styrofoam cup with black coffee. He doesn't look at me as he tears open a packet of Domino sugar and sprinkles a bit into his cup. Too bad there's no hint of sweetness beneath his dark and handsome exterior!

Or is there? His eyes were so kind when he soothed me by the lakeside, folding my wolfishness back into me with hands as gentle as a surgeon's.

"That *kiss*," I hiss so that the crew members milling around cannot hear.

"It was in the script." Dominic meets my eyes over the brim of his cup as he takes a measured sip. "Or did you not read it?"

"*That* was practically necking," I counter. I want to slap the cup out of his hand, but instead, I clench my fists at my sides. "You ruined the take."

Dominic simply shrugs. "You weren't complaining at the time, Flora. Plus, it's good for your career. Isn't your whole *thing* riding on my coattails?"

When we take our marks again, Dominic looks like the cat who ate the canary. He thinks he's rattled me. He has, but I won't give him the satisfaction of seeing it. Instead, when Otto says "Action," I offer him a placid kiss, my body as pliable as a mannequin. I imagine my skin is hard and plasticky, and it's easier to ignore how Dominic's touch makes my skin prickle.

"Cut!" Otto groans. "Let's do that again. Let me see the passion I saw the first time."

The next take is no better than the one that preceded it. "Jesus, it's like watching my grandparents kiss," he groans. "Marks, and *action!*"

Dominic doesn't wait for me to deliver my line. Instead, he abruptly kisses me, his big paw cupping the back of my neck. His thumb presses into the sensitive spot just behind my ear, and I gasp. I forget to count the seconds, my palms alighting on his chest. Through his thin shirt, I feel his heartbeat—slow and steady, as if taking my breath away is no more taxing than taking a leisurely stroll.

When he presses me back into the firm mattress, our hips slot together as if we are mid-tango. Dimly, I hear Otto shout "Cut," then Dominic's weight is gone. He is in video village conversing with an assistant before I even find the breath to sit up.

Chapter Fifteen
(OTTO)

———◁◆▷———

I find myself watching Flora Wright, searching for any sign of what Paul inadvertently caught on camera. When she delivers her lines, I stare at her teeth, expecting to see a sharp canine or saw-toothed incisor. Except, they are all perfectly square and straight, made luminously white by peroxide baked in at 150 degrees.

I encourage her to gesticulate with her hands even in scenes that don't warrant it, wanting to compare the length of her ring and middle fingers. Both hands are perfectly standard, the nails oval shaped.

All I see is an unsure twenty-something girl, her talent smoldering beneath the surface. There's no monster there. Perhaps Paul was right, and the stretch of her jaw on film was simply a ghost in the machine.

It should be a relief. But Robert Taneca's words continue to beleaguer me despite my every attempt to shut them out. *Shoot them first. If you wait, it'll be too late.*

The one thing I can't do is look into her eyes. When I have to speak to her, I look anywhere else: her mouth, her hands, the empty air above her right shoulder, her downy earlobe decorated with a gold button earring. I fear that if I see a hint of incandescence, I'll be forced to take action for the greater good. *Right between the fucking eyes.*

"Mr. Lang?" Stan Chesterfield trots after me as I climb the stairs to my closet-sized office. He's still holding his paper pad in his fist, his pencil tucked inside the coil binding. "Can I get a few minutes of your time?" he huffs.

I stop midway up the metal stairwell, turning to look down at the red-faced reporter. There's a sheen of sweat on his high brow and jowly cheeks. He's either not used to the California heat, or he's well on his way to a heart attack.

Either is bad news for me. If he dies on my set, it'll be the opening line of every movie review. "Lang's latest feature is to die for!" Or "The two-hour run-time will make you wish you were dead!" If he isn't a California native, *Daily Variety* sent a reporter who originally hailed from some podunk gazette in Wichita, or worse, *The New York Times*. In 1944, the *Times* published an article about me called "Creep, Charlatan, or Clever?: The Man Behind *Crazed*."

"I'm a very busy man," I reply testily.

"The studio—" Stan coughs wetly into his fist, and his face turns purple and wrinkly like an overripe beet-root. "They promised an exclusive with you."

Ah, Metro-Goldwyn-Fucking-Mayer, forever the thorn in my side! First, they saddle me with Dominic

Valentine, and now they are promising quotes to shit-stirrers and mudslingers. "Fine," I grumble. "Come on up." I take the remaining stairs two at a time and stride purposefully into my office midway down the catwalk.

Since returning from the lakeside set, my office has become a catchment for the detritus of my rapidly unraveling life. I've been spending most of my time holed up in here, and it shows. There's no time to hide the pile of clothes stashed in the corner, worn and re-worn, nor the dog-eared books and half-unraveled film reels scattered upon every conceivable surface. Since meeting Robert Taneca and the creature in his shed, I have been doing more research, searching for any clue that will implicate—or exonerate—my film's leading lady.

Stan enters the office a moment after I slump into my chair, wiping his brow with a handkerchief embroidered with his initials: SLC. *Hopefully his parents gave him a perfectly horrible middle name, like Leslie.* There's no place for him to sit and no room for a second chair in the small room, so he stands awkwardly beside my desk. He's clearly waiting for me to offer him my seat, but I don't take the bait. Surely, MGM didn't promise him *that!*

"It looks like you've been doing a lot of research," Stan observes, tilting his head to read the spine of a thick, leatherbound tome. "*A Sordid History of Lycanthropy*," he reads. He mispronounces the word as leek-an-thrawpy.

"Is it so surprising that a writer *reads*?" I ask as Stan picks up the book and leafs through it. He shows me a linocut print of a witch—hooked nose, wart, peasant blouse, and all—riding a wolf with a strangely human-like visage.

"*Don't Look in the Lake!* isn't really a monster movie, is it? If anything, the script reads like a criticism of scientific experimentation and the Cold War." He leans his hip onto my desk, and I want to push him off.

"It's a monster movie. There's a monster in it," I say with a laugh. I let him marinate in my non-answer, fishing a cigarette from my breast pocket and putting the filter between my lips. *Where is my lighter?* I push aside a stack of film reels—copies of *The Lodger, Black Friday, The Cabinet of Dr. Caligari,* and *Häxan*—finding my metal Zippo behind them. It takes two tries for the lighter to spark, which feels wholly embarrassing under the eye of the *Daily Variety* lackey.

"Monster movies have sort of fallen out of favor, haven't they? They aren't what audiences find frightening anymore." Despite making himself comfortable on my desk, Stan continues to fidget. He twirls his nub of a pencil between his fingers, taps the eraser against his lips, and tucks and retucks it behind his ear.

"Who told you that?"

"The Box Office," he replies dryly. "Frankly, they don't make money, not in the year of our Lord 1954. That brings me to my follow up question: do you think you'll be able to have the same success as with *Crazed,* or are you chasing ghosts?"

Stan Chesterfield smiles at me. It's a smug smile, as though he's caught me with my hand in the cookie jar. "I'm making a movie that I'm proud of," I say slowly, trying to keep my tone neutral. If I get angry, it'll appear in the article. *Just as we thought, dear reader: Otto J. Lang is a creep with an anger problem!*

Stan chews on that quote and the eraser end of his pencil. "What's leek-an-thrawpy?"

"*Lyncanthropy*," I correct him. "The transformation of a person into a wolf."

"Like a werewolf?" he asks. I nod. He tilts his head to examine more of my books, and I catch a glimpse of a bald spot on the top of his head. "Most of these are about werewolves. Please don't tell me your monster is a Wolf Man, Lang. We've been inundated with that garbage for a decade: *The Wolf Man, Frankenstein Meets the Wolf Man, The House of Frankenstein, The House of Dracula, Abbott and Costello Meet Frankenstein.*" He rattles them off on his fingers, spitting out every syllable as though they are as tart as a piece of lemon hard candy.

"No," I say with a sigh. "It's an amalgamation of a few different monsters. I like to think I chose the scariest parts of each." The slimy, pitted skin of a Gill-Man; the frightening charisma of Dracula; the slow-boiling madness of The Invisible Man; and yes—yes!—the teeth, claws, and murderous impulses of Wolf Man.

"So, you're recycling what worked for Universal. Surely, you understand that makes you look *washed-up*, unoriginal, and uninspired. What was it? Fear that you'll never top *Crazed* and the Academy Award?"

I fantasize about picking up the heavy tome and beating him over the head with it. If I'm enthusiastic enough, surely it will crack his skull like an egg, causing runny, albumic cerebrospinal fluid to leak out of his nose. I imagine him pleading for me to stop, his voice shrill and quavering. *I didn't mean it*, he'd whine, *you are gifted—your ideas are avant-garde!*

"Mr. Lang?" Stan Chesterfield claps his hand on my shoulder, giving me a shake. "Are you alright? Your eyes went a little glassy."

I shake off his touch. "I was trying to decide how to politely respond to your asinine question," I mutter. "No, I don't think I'm being unoriginal, and, *no*, I'm not worried about failing. If I was, I would have just made *Crazed II*."

"Let's switch gears. Can you comment about the cast? There are some who think hiring a nobody and Hollywood's disillusioned son was the wrong move. Some speculate their relationship is overshadowing the film."

I chuckle. "'Some' meaning 'Stan Chesterfield of *Daily Variety*,' I imagine." I think of the kiss between Dominic and Flora on set, the smoldering fire within turning their faces rosy. It was the very kiss I was promised in their screen test months ago. It's a kiss that, if shown in the trailer, will put butts in seats. "I have every confidence in my stars. Now, if you'll excuse me, I have to get back to work. Surely, I've fulfilled MGM's promise to the magazine."

Stan sighs, tucking his pencil back into the spiral binding of his notebook. "Fine," he acquiesces. "Thank you for your time, Mr. Lang." He finally deigns to heft his bulk off my desk, and I push my books back into the empty space so he can't nest there again like the haughty chanticleer he thinks he is.

But Stan Chesterfield doesn't immediately move toward the door. Instead, he picks up two more of my books, silently reading the titles. In his right hand, he holds *Shapeshifters in Myth,* and in the left, *Un Histoire de Loups Garous*. "Y'know, this seems like more than a passing interest," he muses more so to himself than me. "An 'amalgamation of a few different monsters', my ass! D'ya have a hard-on for Lon Chaney or something? I mean, he's a handsome man—lacking in the tits department, though."

"Goodbye, Mr. Chesterfield," I snarl through my teeth, snatching the books from his hands. "Good luck with your puff piece. I'm sure you'll get promoted to current affairs in no time."

Chapter Sixteen
(DOMINIC)

————◁◆▷————

"I can't believe you convinced me to do this," I groan, setting my whisky tumbler on the mantle of the fireplace. The amber liquid sloshes in the glass, and a few droplets fall upon the pristine limestone. I've never lit a fire in the hearth, the weather never gets quite cold enough, but there are several ring-shaped water stains from champagne flutes, highball glasses, and the like.

"It's the kind thing to do," Penelope replies. "You only have a week left on set. You may as well show your appreciation." She takes a sip of Claret, the pale ruby liquid a near-match to her lipstick. Tonight, she is wearing a teal hostess-style gown with a high slit revealing tight cigarette pants beneath, and her hair is pulled back into a high, sleek ponytail. It's an ensemble meant to tantalize me, but I'm too irritated to take the bait.

My living room is crowded, the cast and crew of *Don't Look in the Lake!* commingling. I find myself staring at a man I recognize as a gaffer sitting on my pristine couch, the remains of his shrimp cocktail staining his shirt lapel. There's even a gnawed-on shrimp tail half-tucked into his breast pocket. I think that I would rather send my appreciation to Scotch-Guard. "I shouldn't have let you talk me into it," I grumble.

Penelope just flashes me a coquettish smile. "Everyone is having a great time. Why can't you?"

I down the remainder of my whisky, a fiery mix of oak, malt, and toasted almond. As the warmth spreads through my belly and loosens my extremities, I wonder how many more glasses I need to drink to have a good time. "I'm going to get another drink," I tell my companion, heading into the kitchen.

I am almost taller than the arched doorways, and I have to duck to keep from damaging my heavily moussed quaff. The Spanish-style kitchen is large, and in the daytime, is full of sunlight from the many windows. But now, it's dim, lit only by the heavy, wrought-iron Spanish chandelier hanging above the dining alcove. It doesn't quite match the kitchen's airy atmosphere nor color scheme, but Penny fell in love with it at the Paramount Swap Meet.

It's quiet here; most of the guests are in the living room, and the bow-tied caterers are making their rounds, arms laden with platters of bacon-wrapped sausage, salmon mousse canapés, deviled eggs, stuffed mushrooms, and tiny glass bowls of fruit compote. The counters are crowded with soiled Fiestaware mixing bowls, a handheld ice crusher, various utensils, a roasting pan, a cast iron skillet with a thick layer of grease congealing at the bottom, and a half-empty bottle of cooking Sherry. I certainly hope the caterers will clean this up.

I skirt around the kitchen island to find the chef kneeling with his head in the oven.

He has the right idea, I think wryly before realizing he is merely examining whether the meringue on the baked Alaska had browned evenly. Seemingly satisfied, Chef Russo—*is that his name?*—removes the dessert from the oven and sets it on the stovetop. The stiff tips of the fluffy meringue remind me of the spines of an agitated pufferfish dragged from the depths of the Pacific.

"We'll cut this in *pochi minuti*, Signore Valentine," he tells me in a thick accent I think may be Italian. He must think I've come to complain about the service.

"That's fine," I assure him, holding up my glass. "I'm only coming to get a drink."

"Is no one manning the bar?" he asks, his thick eyebrows knitting together.

"I like to pour my own," I assure him, noting the passionate quaver in his voice and a sudden ruddiness in his craggy cheeks. I expect he is considering rushing into the living room to scream at his staff on my behalf ("Teste di legno, cani inutili, tutti voi!"). Seemingly relieved, Chef Russo returns to his work, humming over the dessert as though it's a colicky baby.

My brass-and-glass bar cart is on the far side of the kitchen, butting up against the hacienda window looking out at the pool and backyard. I am immediately aware of a square-shaped bit of empty space the decanter of L.W. Harper Bourbon had once occupied.

"Somebody is cruisin' for a bruisin'," I grumble. Clearly, someone from the crew snatched it up. Maybe it's hidden beneath the ugly, pinstriped sport coat that Mr. Shrimp Cocktail had draped over the armrest! I wouldn't put it past him. I'm certain I've seen him sneaking nibbles off the cast's craft services table.

Not wanting to return to the party empty-handed, or particularly sober, I settle for gin. I don't bother getting ice from the fridge; it'll only water it down. As the taste of juniper settles on my tongue—equal parts piney, honeyed, and tart—I stare idly out into the dark backyard. The pool lights cast a bluish glow over the Laurel trees and the fence line beyond.

A woman is sitting on the pool edge, her feet in the water. My missing bottle of bourbon rests beside her hip. From this angle, I can't quite see who it is. Covertly, I ease open the back door, stepping out onto the patio. The woman doesn't seem to hear me as I approach. She picks up the glass bottle by the neck and takes a swig directly from it. "It's rude to steal from your host," I call.

The woman sputters and coughs. "Oh!" she exclaims once she has regained her breath. I recognize the voice, having been forced to hear it nearly every day for the last three months. *Flora.* She looks up at me, the pool's glow making her appear alienish. "I didn't think you'd notice."

Flora is wearing a boat-necked dress, and I find myself staring at the constellation of freckles on her bare shoulder. The full skirt is shucked up around her thighs to avoid getting the hem wet in the chlorinated water. Despite being caught red-handed, she takes another measured sip from the bottle. "Do you want some?" she asks.

I should snatch away the bottle and head inside. But I don't want to return to the party. Besides, it's a beautiful night. In early September, nightfall often brings with it a pleasant breeze that cools the sweat on one's skin. And there's something quite beguiling about Flora tonight—a lackadaisical energy very unlike her typically buttoned-up exterior. Perhaps it's the bourbon.

I slip my shoes off, roll up my starched pant legs, and sit on the pool deck beside her. When I plunge my legs in, I am surprised at how cool the water is. It makes me hiss, gooseflesh prickling up my calves and making the thick hair there stand on end. I gulp the last of my gin then refill my glass with the dark bourbon. I place the bottle on my right side, so she can't easily reach it.

"I never would have thought you'd throw a party," Flora says, "and certainly not one so *normal*."

I laugh. "What do you mean?"

"Well, the tabloids make it sound as though you spend every evening leaping out the windows at the Chateau and getting into brawls at the Mocambo. I didn't expect a caterer and jazz music." She laughs, throwing her head back as though it's the funniest thing in the world.

"This is all Penelope's doing. I much prefer the Frolic Room and drinking with Howard Hughes."

"Liar. Howard Hughes is a known teetotaler," she snickers. She reaches across my lap to snag the decanter and tips it back to take a hearty swallow.

Then, she holds it between her knees, tapping her nails on the faceted spout. It sounds vaguely like the melody to *I Love Lucy*.

"I'm much more of a cube than the tabloids make me out to be," I admit. "Though, I *did* once punch Errol Flynn for chatting up my date at the Mocambo." I flex my hand, showing her the flat, white scar on my knuckle, courtesy of Errol's wedge-shaped chin.

"Penelope Cox?" Flora asks, giving me a sidelong look.

"It was years before Penny." I cast a glance back toward the house as if expecting to see her face in the window. But Penny won't look for me; she's relishing her role as hostess, no doubt. I can almost picture her holding court, a plate of canapes balanced atop her fingertips. She'll be telling stories now, in which I'll feature heavily as her louche beau. Champagne loosens her tongue, and inevitably, lies spill out. It's a large part of why our relationship fizzled. Or rather, imploded in truly spectacular fashion.

A champagne flute explodes above the fireplace mantle, glass tinkling upon the hearth. I hop away, shaking my head. "You're incorrigible," I say and laugh because the alternative is clenching my fists. Paying her no mind, I loosen my tie and drape it over the banister to take upstairs later.

Penelope's face is as red as a Haniya mask, her teeth squealing as she gnashes her jaw. "You can't tell me who to talk to," she spits. Despite being slight, she cuts an imposing figure, especially in the full-skirted cocktail gown she'd worn to the premiere of

The Cattlemen *earlier in the evening. It makes her look like an agitated peacock, feathers akimbo.*

"I can if you're talking about me. *You do know who that was, right?" I had stewed about what I had seen for the entirety of the film screening and the car ride home afterward: Penelope leaning close to a man in the hallway during intermission, letting him light her cigarette. Their fingers touched, and they laughed as if sharing a secret.*

"He's a friend," she says with a groan. "Or am I not allowed to have friends, Dominic?" Her pale eyebrow arches. She thinks I'm jealous.

"A friend!" I scoff. "He's a muck-raker for Confidential. *The very same one who wrote that article saying we had a ménage à trois with Leena."*

"We did," *Penny exclaims, throwing up her hands in exasperation.*

"And how did Confidential *find out, hm?" I ask, nearly spitting the words. They taste sour on my tongue—poisonous. Tonight, when I saw them together, it was as though someone had turned on the prover-bial lights, leaving me blinking and overwhelmed by my surroundings. The source in the article, described only as a "close, personal friend of Dominic Valentine" was the one person who should never have divulged my secrets.*

"You should be thanking me." Penny unceremo-niously plops on the couch, her skirt a puff of bro-cade and taffeta around her. She reaches within the folds of fabric to remove her Roger Vivier heels and tosses them beneath the coffee table. "The Korean War

ends, yet all anyone can talk about is what a lucky man you are!"

I snort. *"It was an invasion of my—our—privacy."* *Without preamble, I head upstairs, not wanting to look at her anymore. I am dimly aware of the swish-a-swish of fabric as she follows me into our bedroom, but I ignore her. I just want to go to bed. I unbutton my dress shirt and slither out of my slacks, leaving the lot in a puddle on the cream, broadloom carpet.*

"Unzip me?" Penelope asks, turning so I can see the zipper that runs from mid-back to the cleft of her buttocks. I sigh, doing as she asks. The dress is borrowed from Balmain, and if I don't help, she'll simply cut herself out of it with kitchen shears, leaving me to deal with the fallout. That's Penelope's style: light a match to admire the flame then toss it aside when it becomes too hot. I am always extinguishing fires. Whatever she's said to the tabloid reporter tonight will be just another blaze.

Just. *I'm making excuses.*

My knuckle bumps along her knobby vertebrae as I pull down the zipper. When the fabric gapes, she steps out of it, revealing a thigh-length silk slip in a blush pink. I drape the dress over an armchair, trying, in vain, to smooth the wrinkles on the bodice with my palms. "I'm only trying to help you," Penny murmurs, keen to keep the discussion going.

"You're trying to help yourself, Pen," I growl, whirling on her. "I'm starting to think this is just a game to you—a means to an end."

Penelope's crimson lip quirks. I'm not sure if she's trying to swallow a sneer or a sob. Without a word, she

storms into the Master Bathroom and turns on the tap
to full blast. I follow and hover in the doorway, nei-
ther coming nor going. She plunges her hands beneath
the stream then begins to scrub the makeup off her
face with her palms. Her movements are overwrought,
as though she's on stage under a spotlight, miming
for an audience. With her mascara running down her
teardrop-shaped face, she glares at my reflection in
the mirror.

"How dare you?" Her voice is barely discernible
over the still-running tap. The sink fills with water
made cloudy by her makeup. The color reminds me of
the dusty Dakota plains where I filmed The Cattlemen.
It was a heavy place where one couldn't help but speak
in a hushed tone. It was as though the steppes were the
nave of a cathedral and the hills on the horizon were
its pulpit. I feel some of that heaviness now.

"The water is going to overflow," I observe coolly,
gesturing at the sink.

"Is that all you have to say?" Penelope's voice
breaks, and she weeps unabashedly. "You accuse me
of using you, and now, all you care about is the fucking
linoleum?" She slaps her palms on the porcelain but
still doesn't close the faucet.

I lean against the doorjamb, crossing my arms over
my naked chest. "Since we started dating, you've made
out like gangbusters, haven't you? I'm only calling it
like I see it, doll." I dress my words up in the regalia
of bravado to avoid sounding hurt. "In the last four
months, you've become a media darling. The tab-
loids can't get enough, you got that contract with Max

Factor, and it's all because you've been telling sala-cious stories about me."

The water breaches the sink basin, soaking the floor. "Golly, you're arrogant," Penelope exclaims. She doesn't seem to notice the water lapping against her bare feet. "I don't need to ride your coat-tails, Dominic."

I laugh. "Could have fooled me. I want you out of my fucking house." Her face seems to crack in twain at my ultimatum, her mouth agape. A sob, plaintive and pathetic, erupts from her chest, and she stumbles as if I punched her in the gut.

"You're making a mistake," she wails.

I finally step into the bathroom and shut the faucet off. Penelope looks up into my face, hopeful, but I avoid her blue eyes. "I'm sleeping in the other room," I say coldly. "I want you out first thing tomorrow." She doesn't pursue me across the hall. But as I crawl into the guest bed, the sheets faintly fusty from disuse, I hear her scream, and something heavy shatters the mirror.

"I've been working up the courage to introduce myself," Flora admits, interrupting my woolgathering. "*A Perfect Stranger* is one of my favorite films."

I snort. "Haven't you realized by now that actors are cut from the same cloth as everyone else? Penelope Cox is just as insecure and unsure of herself as you are. More so because she cares what those nobodies inside think of her." I take the bottle from Flora's grip, and our fingers touch. Hers are chilly as though she just thrust them into an icebox.

"What makes you think I don't?" Flora asks, raising her eyebrows. The blue light from the pool plays across her cheekbones, making her appear less than corporeal. I nearly convince myself that if I touched her face, my fingers would slide right through her. Would it feel like putting one's hand too close to a staticky television screen in need of degaussing?

"Well, you're skulking around in my backyard."

"I'm sitting, not skulking. It's just—" She hesitates, sucking her tongue between her teeth. "Why are you being kind to me?"

I take three quick gulps from the decanter, and the heat of the liquor floods my extremities. It's quite pleasant, like stepping into the embrace of a parent or lover. "I'm nice," I reply, unable to contain the defensiveness in my voice.

Flora laughs and pulls her legs out of the pool. Carefully, she rises, adjusting her skirt over her damp calves. "You *aren't* nice, Valentine." She turns toward the house but doesn't move. "Why did you kiss me?" she finally asks, looking down at me. Her jaw is a right angle.

The kiss! It was meant to be a lark, nothing more. I wanted to rattle her, to wipe the smug, holier-than-thou expression off her pretty face. I wanted to see whether she would falter, stumble, give an inch. Except, when I kissed her, it was like drinking a gallon of bourbon straight from the barrel. I felt equal parts feverish and heady, and I wanted to keep the inevitable hangover at bay. It took everything in me to listen when Otto called "cut" because I wanted to drink her down until there were only suds left in the bottom of the glass.

God, even now, the thought of it makes my cock stir in my slacks.

"It was in the script," I reply, easily. A bald-faced lie.

Flora huffs and heads toward the house. She is careful on the slate paving stones in her bare feet; they'll be slick. I turn my gaze back toward the pool and spot her heels. She left them behind. "Flora," I call, grabbing them and scrambling to my feet. My costar pauses, her fingertips alighting on the door handle. "Your heels—"

Flora looks at her bare feet then at the winklepicker heels dangling from my crooked fingers. "Oh!" she exclaims. She waits as I pad across the patio then takes the shoes from my outstretched hand. When she bends to slip them on, she loses her balance and grabs my arm for support. It's the first time she's touched me without being told to. When the script calls for it, she touches me with fingers as soft as a moth's wings, always ready to pull away as if I'm in danger of igniting. But now, her grip on my arm is unyielding, my shirt wrinkling.

"Sorry," she murmurs when she finally straightens, both heels moored on their respective feet. It takes her a moment longer to realize she's still touching me, and she jerks her hand behind her back with another chirruped apology.

This close to the mansion, I can vaguely hear the sounds of the party; "Sh-Boom" by The Crew-Cuts is playing on the record player, hundreds of voices talk in unison, and I swear I can hear Penelope's voice above the din. She's singing along, I think, her breathy mezzo-soprano following the melody like a roadmap. I picture her sashaying around the room, drink in hand, unabashedly flirting with the guests. She always loved being the center of attention, and I was the perfect billboard for her act. *Who is that draped on Dominic Valentine's arm?*

Suddenly, the thought of returning to the party is next to unbearable. "Flora, go for a run with me."

"You can't leave your own party," Flora says with a chuckle, pulling the door open. Now, I can truly hear Penelope, her singing voice breathy and weak thanks to a near-decade of Pall Mall cigarettes. Someone whoops. The kitchen is crowded now too. Many of the cater waiters linger there, bow ties askew, washing dishes at the sink or surreptitiously picking at leftovers. Chef Russo barks orders in a mix of English and Italian—"Sbrigati! Pack it up!" I push the door shut.

"It's Penelope's party. Come on—run with me. Please."

Flora looks up into my face as if my intentions are written there. "Are you playing a joke on me?"

I unbutton my crisp, white, dress shirt, taking her non-answer as a yes. "Come on," I urge, "before anyone sees."

CHAPTER SEVENTEEN
(FLORA)

---◁◆▷---

Shirt half-buttoned, Dominic leads me past the pool and behind the small pool house. There's a cabana there, draped in off-white muslin. The area is well-hidden from prying eyes. I hadn't even seen the small hut from the house. Beneath the fabric plafond, complete with a gaudy chandelier at its apex, are two over-stuffed lounge chairs, a small brick oven, and a bar cart similar to the one in the kitchen.

Dominic shrugs off his shirt and tosses it onto one of the lounge chairs. I find myself staring at the long, tapered lines of his back. A heart-shaped mole adorns the plane of his shoulder blade. Then, he unceremoniously pulls down his pants. Embarrassed, I yelp, slapping my hands over my eyes. Dominic snickers. "Haven't you run with other wolves before?"

"Y-y-yes," I stammer. I've seen Rafe, Elton, and Nico naked before. Ama and Mags too. Nudity doesn't often warrant a second glance. But with Dominic, it feels wholly different. We lack the easygoing, intimate relationship of friends, and instead, walk the fine line between enemies and ... something else entirely. It's as though there are two Dominics: the arrogant actor, and the man who oozes sorrow and looks to me for comfort. Isn't that why he kissed me so passionately? The journalist from *Daily Variety* made him feel off-balance, so he made certain I felt it too.

A loud *cra-a-ack* makes me uncover my eyes, and I find Dominic on his hands and the balls of his feet, his vertebrae pushing against his taut skin. He's entirely naked now, his buttocks clenched as the pain of transformation washes through him. It comes in waves, like contractions; sometimes you can just catch your breath before your ribs flare, or your metatarsal bones pop, pop, pop! While he is distracted, I swiftly undress and drape my dress, slip, and lingerie over the adjacent lounge chair.

I fall forward onto my hands as the red wolf pulls her leash from between my fingers. I flex my fingers into the earthen floor of the cabana, packing dirt under my lengthening fingernails. I find myself watching Dominic as my body spasms, my vision tunneling into pinpoints. He has regained his composure and sits back on his haunches, his long, pink tongue lolling out of his mouth. His fur is dark but not quite black. It is the shade of dark chocolate, damp soil, and the bark of a black walnut tree. His head is angular, dolichocephalic like a borzoi's. It gives him a sort of regal air, which suits him.

"Are you alright?" he asks as a reedy whine escapes my throat. His voice is hoarse, a half-octave lower than his normal baritone. Painstakingly, I clamber to my feet, shaking out my fur.

"I'm out of practice," I reply, embarrassed. I was born wolfish, and the pain doesn't typically rattle me. But I haven't worn my fur since flying to Los Angeles. It's akin to running a decathlon after being sedentary.

Dominic, for once, doesn't pick at my scab. Instead, he says, "C'mon!" and heads away from the mansion toward a line of identical-looking shrubs. Each has been trimmed into an oblong shape with rounded edges. Dominic squeezes between two shrubs, and I follow the brush-like end of his tail through the mire of curved branches and needle-like leaves. I expect to reach a privacy fence on the other side, but there isn't one. Instead, we are ejected out onto a winding, unmarked road with steep canyon walls on the far side. Chaparral vegetation covers the sloping landscape, each evergreen plant more bristly than its neighbor. It looks both inhospitable and beautiful, like an alien planet.

As casually as though we are taking a midnight stroll, Dominic walks along the roadside. We pass his neighbors' backyards, all fenced with shrubbery and, on one occasion, a wrought iron fence with sharp spikes capping every post. A large pitbull slams his muscular shoulders against the bars, thick globules of saliva puddling the ground as he snarls. We pay him no mind. There are no streetlights, but our feet fall sure.

The street dead-ends, and we head uphill. In the distance, I hear a cacophony of yips and shrieks — coyotes. They won't approach us. While there are certainly more of them, we are much larger. Even with their peanut-sized brains, they know an unfair fight when they see one.

"This is my favorite spot," Dominic says, his long, tapered noise pointing toward the cliff edge of the ravine. Beyond, we have an eagle's eye view of the entirety of Benedict Canyon: roofs of homes ranging from very small to sprawling estates; driveways with switchbacks; steep grades dug by excavators to accommodate pools, jacuzzis, and retaining walls; and on the horizon, the glittering lights of Los Angeles proper.

Dominic sits back on his haunches near the cliff edge, and I settle beside him, laying sphinx-like on my belly. The steep drop makes me feel dizzy, but I can see why it's his favorite. It's an entirely different view of the bustling city. From here, you can't smell the engine exhaust, stale urine, nor the rotting flowers sold from panhandler's carts. No one is looking at us through a lens, asking for a smile, a quote, or a moment of faux intimacy. It's the first time I've seen it as beautiful rather than a concrete metropolis wherein glitz is currency.

"I was telling the truth, you know," I murmur, not taking my eyes off the horizon. The velvety night sky is hazy with pollution, but if I squint, I can just make out a few of the brightest stars.

"About what?"

"I never gave the tabloid those quotes about us. My team planted them," I say. Dominic doesn't reply, merely shifts his weight to rest his pointy elbow upon his knee. For a long moment, we sit in silence, the only sounds our asynchronous breathing and the breeze ruffling the sage brush.

"Penelope used to plant stories about me — us. She would call the papers before leaving my house so that the cameras would be outside waiting. I was blind to it for so long because I loved her. I thought you were doing the same thing, but," he chuckles, showing rows of teeth, "you didn't even have the decency to fuck me first."

"Are you still together?" I ask curiously.

"Absolutely not. But once in a blue moon, we spend the night together. Or, like tonight, she meddles in my career because she thinks she's the one responsible if I fail." He shrugs, a bizarrely human gesture in a body without the means for it. It looks more like he's trying to scratch an itch he can't reach. "After she and I broke up, I went off the deep end. I'm sure you've heard about it."

Dominic Valentine's name is never written without an adjective preceding it. *The troubled Dominic Valentine. The volatile Dominic Valentine. The irritable Domonic Valentine.* He famously attacked a reporter outside of his home the morning after *The Cattlemen* premiere. There's a photo of the incident: Dominic, disheveled and shoeless, swinging his fist at a cowering man. The man was holding his camera aloft as a shield, but the lens was already broken and dangling from the first punch. "I know," I whisper.

Suddenly, there's a scream from behind us. It's loud, reverberating through the canyon. Surely, the power of it shredded the screamer's vocal cords, rendering their throat raw. I turn, expecting to see a woman in extreme distress. But the creature standing several yards away from us is a mountain lion, her half-moon shaped ears pinned back against her round skull. She stands with her head hung low, her muscular haunches taut like springs.

We've inadvertently intruded on her home.

The territorial mountain lion screams again and lunges at us. Dominic pushes me out of the way and grasps the feline's snout, pushing it up and back. Despite his size, her aggression makes her a worthy adversary. She swipes at him with sharp claws, bloodying his chest. "Run!" he yells, but I feel rooted in place. The mountain lion and wolf tussle on the cliff edge, dislodging the loose rocks and soil. Pebbles *plink, plink, plonk* down the precipitous rock face.

The mountain lion's unrelenting attack loosens Dominic's grip on her maw, and she ducks beneath his palm with the grace of a featherweight prizefighter. I am suddenly cognizant of how out of our depth we are. Each movement she makes is calculated, not an ounce of energy is wasted. She's made to fight—to kill. It is coded into every nerve, seeping into her bone marrow. Conversely, we are slowed by our ostensibly human nature. Before the mountain lion can open another trench in Dominic's profusely bleeding chest, I slam into her, throwing her off her feet. It's reckless, putting us both too close to the cliff's crumbling edge.

The ground disappears from beneath me. My stomach drops with it, reminding me of the time I rode the Coney Island Cyclone, cutting half-moons into Ama's arm as we took the first drop. I find myself looking down at the tops of trees and the mountain lion's wide eyes as she twists into a knot in midair. *I'm going to die,* I think, preternaturally calm.

Something roughly grasps my arm, and I collide with the cliff wall. *Oomph*. All of the air jettisons from my lungs, and black motes burst before my eyes. "I've got you!" Dominic shouts, heaving me up. Without any breath, I can't tell him that it feels like every tendon in my arm is tearing. With a grunt, he drags me back onto solid ground. Finally, I am able to inflate my lungs. The influx of oxygen is euphoric, and I let out a short, humorless guffaw.

On his knees beside me, Dominic touches my face. "You saved me," he murmurs. The fur upon his chest looks glossy in the starlight, damp with clotting blood. It reminds me of the faux skin he wears as the monster on set. If I touch it, will it have the give of foam rubber beneath my fingertips?

"She was going to kill you," I say, each syllable punctuated by a little giggle. There's nothing funny about this, but it's better than crying. I fear if I let myself cry, I'll inevitably drown in my tears. Moments ago, I was looking directly into the void, and I had accepted it because I had no choice in the matter. Was that what it had been like for Nico, with Elton's whole fist inside his gut? Did the more primal part of his brain simply turn off the fear and pain, leaving him only with a casual sense of curiosity? *Oh, I think I'm dying. I wonder how long this will take.*

For a moment, it looks as though Dominic's face is melting as each strand of his fur is sucked into its respective pore, revealing unblemished skin. His snout flattens, crumpling like a Coca-Cola can. The pain makes him pant, and I watch his teeth become blunt and square. Just as his clavicle is wrenched askew,

jerking his shoulders like a marionette, I close my eyes.
I can't bear to watch any more.

This time, my own metamorphosis comes easy.
The shock of my near-death experience makes the pain
feel like a celebration. *I am so blissfully alive!*

When I open my eyes, Dominic is looking down at
me, his bushy eyebrows knitted together in concern—
or is it pain? Without his fur, the wound on his chest
is visible: a latticework of scratches, the deepest of
which transverses the bottom of his right areola. The
bleeding has started anew, the wound irritated by his
transformation.

"You need to go to the hospital," I say, sitting up.

"How can I possibly explain this?" He snickers.
"I can just see the headline now: 'Dominic Valentine
thinks he's an animal tamer, more on page seven.'"

"We should at least get it cleaned up. Come on." I
clamber to my feet and reach down for his hand. To
my surprise, he doesn't bat it away but allows me to
pull him to his feet. The effort makes him go pale and
breathless, and I thread my arm around his tapered
waist to give him some support. His skin is clammy
against mine, and our bare flesh sticks together. We
have a long walk ahead of us.

We walk in silence, communicating only by
touch—a squeeze to signify comfort, a palm to the
back to say *I know, but we need to walk faster*. Naked
and bleeding, we are exposed out here. The pitbull
barks at us again, and this time, we give him a wide
berth, stepping onto the pebbly asphalt. Dominic wordlessly points out the gap between the hedges, and we
slip through, arms looped as though we are making a

daisy chain. Our humanoid bodies don't fit as neatly in this space, and thin branches painfully whip against my thighs, leaving welts. I am too tired to revel at the casual intimacy between us.

In the cabana, we both dress. I have to help Dominic put on his shirt. The bleeding has stopped again, leaving only specks of red on the white fabric. "Maybe you can say you spilled some wine?" I offer. I button his shirt carefully, aware of his hot breath on my face.

"No one would ever believe that," he says with a snort. "I don't drink wine. I'll just say I'm going to bed early, and no one will be the wiser." Wordlessly, I turn so that he can zip up my dress, and he does so without complaint, his knuckles gliding up between my shoulder blades. His breath is on my shoulder now, his chin dipped toward my ear. "Flora," he says breathlessly. "Come with me. Come to bed with me."

It would be so easy to take his hand and let him lead me up the stairs. I can even imagine his bedroom—sumptuous linens on a four-poster bed, heavy brocade curtains like a Venetian palace, and a jacuzzi tub which could comfortably seat two. It would be exhilarating—touching him, having him touch me—but it would be wrong. We are just coworkers, nothing more. Maybe, with effort, we could be friends, but we aren't that now. Tonight, we are just trauma-bonded, and in the light of morning, we will surely see it as such.

"Goodnight, Dominic," I say, stepping away from him. Outside of the circle of his embrace, my skin prickles with a sudden chill. I wrap my arms around myself, but it does nothing.

Dominic looks at me through hooded eyes. His jaw tightens so much that the vein at his temple pulses. "Suit yourself," he grumbles, obviously hurt. "Goodnight, Miss Wright." Turning on his heel, he strides across the lawn, stopping briefly at the pool's edge to grab the decanter of bourbon. I wonder if the bottle will be his bedfellow tonight. Or will it be Penelope Cox?

Dominic's mouth crushes mine, and he tastes like bourbon. I feel heady too, as though we've gone drink for drink.

Cool hands find the zipper at the back of my dress, pulling it down to its terminus just above the waistband of my underwear. The fabric of the bodice gapes open, falling down around my waist. Shadows dapple my bare skin in the shape of maple leaves, a vine of tattoos from shoulder to belly button. Somewhere, I hear a seagull cry, which doesn't make sense. We aren't at the seaside, are we?

Dominic cups my breasts through my bra, and I find myself arching my back so that I fill his palms. "Look at her," he exclaims when he breaks our kiss. "She wants this so badly."

Who is he talking to?

Dominic tugs down the cups of my bra, freeing my breasts. When he sucks my nipple between his teeth, liquid heat pools between my legs. He lavishes one nipple with his tongue, and he tweaks the other between his thumb and forefinger. I twist strands of his hair around my fingers like horse's reins, encouraging his ministrations. Yes!

It takes me a moment to realize that the fingers unhooking my bra aren't his. They are softer and gentler. I crane my neck and look into the ocean blue eyes of Penelope Cox. Oh!

While I watch, she presses her lips against my bare shoulder, leaving behind a perfect lipstick mark. "She wants us so badly," *Penelope concurs.*

Do I? I admire Penelope. I've spent hours squinting into the mirror, trying to emulate the pointed arch and blunted tail of her brow. I tried, in vain, to save up for a Hermés clutch because I saw her carrying one. She grins at me, planting a kiss upon the side of my mouth, and my stomach twists.

Dominic, tiring of my breasts, kisses Penelope. I am pinned between their bodies but not forgotten. They both run their hands over my naked breasts and back, touching me with the gusto with which I expect they touch each other. Someone tugs down what remains of my dress, and I am aware then that both of my lovers are naked too. Dominic's cock rests against my stomach, precum dribbling.

The three of us lay on an impossibly soft bed, the pillows stuffed with goose down. When I look upward, I expect to see the ceiling, but it's as though it has been sheared off the room altogether. All I see is a canopy of trees and the unblemished, blue sky. There isn't even a single cloud.

"Where are we?" I ask, my voice seeming to float around the room; it comes from within me and outside of me—a chorus of me's.

Chapter Seventeen (Flora)

"Does it matter?" Dominic asks, his hand slipping between my legs.

I suppose it doesn't. Penelope leans in to kiss me, her blond hair falling across my cheek like a curtain. Her kiss is softer than Dominic's—flirtier too. The tip of her tongue taps against mine. I find myself entranced by her unblemished skin; even up close, she is as immaculate as a porcelain doll. The blush upon her apple cheeks looks painted on.

Hesitant, I reach out and cup her breast. I've never touched another girl before—not like this. Her eyes slide closed like a contented cat as I brush the pad of my thumb over her nipple.

The two of us roll so I am astride her narrow hips. She raises her hips to grind against me, and I gasp. The sound makes birds, roosting somewhere in the gnarled branches of the trees above, take flight.

"My girls," Dominic exclaims, his cock in his hand. My girls, my girls, mine, mine, mine…

I wake with a start, throwing off the white comforter. The alarm clock on the bedside table caterwauls. I turn it off with a touch.

It's only 4 a.m., but I'm due on set in an hour and a half. As I get out of bed, I find myself thinking of the dream. It's becoming less delible with every expelled breath. But if I concentrate very hard, I can still feel Dominic's lips on mine and Penelope's silken hair tickling my skin.

There's a knock at the door. "Room service!"

I open the door to find a tray on the carpet. There's a cloche covering the plate and a small mug of steaming coffee—no cream or sugar. I carry the lot to my table, hoping to find something scrumptious under the cloche. But as usual, I find a half-wedge of plain toast and scrambled egg whites. "Thanks, Carver," I grumble.

By the time I've finished my meager breakfast, I can't recall the dream at all.

CHAPTER EIGHTEEN
(OTTO)

⊲◆⊳

On the penultimate day of principal photography, Dominic Valentine refuses to come out of his trailer. Two runners attempt to fetch him but come back in tears. "Fine," I grumble. "I'll get him."

The narrow lanes between the rows of trailers are cool, shaded by flapping awnings. The only exception is when I pass the air conditioning units attached to the vehicles' rears; the fans blast hot air, ruffling my hair. Dominic's trailer is midway down the second row, and I open the door without knocking. "Come on, Valentine," I call as I climb up the stairs. "You're supposed to be in makeup."

It's dark and cool inside like a cave. I blink rapidly to adjust my eyes and make out the broad, nude back of the actor. He's slouching at his dinette table, his head in his hands. "I'm not filming today," he grumbles. "Get out of my trailer."

"Too hungover from your little party last night?" I ask, unable to mask my snide tone. Despite receiving an invitation, I didn't attend. Frankly, there's nothing to celebrate yet. The movie isn't done, and their little get-together is as good as a curse. It's akin to saying *good luck* instead of *break a leg,* forgetting to turn on the ghost light onstage after hours, or uttering "Macbeth" aloud. Surely, I'm not the only one who believes in such superstitions.

"Get out," Dominic snarls. He stands so abruptly that the table wobbles. When he turns to face me, I notice raised lesions crisscrossing his chest, some of which leak a yellowish pus. They are so fresh that the skin around the wounds is still inflamed and, I expect, hot to the touch.

"What happened to you?" I ask, alarmed.

"I got into a fight with my gardener," he deadpans. "You can't pay good help these days." He reaches for a dark shirt tossed upon his couch and pulls it over his head. He winces as he pulls it down over his broad chest.

I want to pry. But I also want to cajole the red-tempered actor into filming his scenes. If we don't, the production will run longer than it already has, and I'll have to ask MGM for more money to keep us afloat. It's degrading. I may as well be getting on my knees before the MGM president, kissing his thighs. *Please sir, can I have another fifteen grand?*

"You have one scene to do today, Valentine. You need to get to the makeup trailer."

Dominic looks as though he wants to hit me. His knuckles blanch. I steel myself for an attack, knowing he outweighs me by at least twenty pounds. With a sigh, he brushes past me in the narrow aisle, stomping down the stairs. He slams the door as he leaves but veers toward the makeup trailer.

Flora doesn't know how to hold a knife.

"Flora, you're going to *stab* him, not carve up a Christmas ham," I groan, grinding the heels of my hands into my eye sockets. I get out of my chair for the second time to adjust her grip on the prop knife's handle. Then, I guide her hand into Dominic's abdomen. The blade compresses into the handle.

Dominic, reclining on the floor atop his mark, rolls his eyes. Flora's cheeks redden, and she fumbles the blade again. "Can't you do anything right?" Dominic exclaims. He may as well have put a *real* knife between Flora's ribs. She chokes out a little sob, frustrated tears springing into her eyes.

"You're not being fair," she snaps.

"Life's not fair, sweetheart," Dominic grouses. He throws his forearm over his eyes as if he's planning to take a cat nap. It's a dismissive gesture. He's done with her, me, and this whole endeavor.

"We're filming it again," I say firmly, feeling as though I'm losing control of my set. It's not something I'm accustomed to. My personal life is the car crash, there's no such foolishness here.

"Now, marks!" I say a little too brusquely. I retreat back to my chair, sitting forward with my elbows on my knees, steepling my fingers beneath my chin.

My assistant holds the clapboard up. "Take fift—," she begins, but suddenly, Dominic is on his feet. Flora, still kneeling, looks up at him, mouth agape.

"I'm done," he announces to the crew. "Film it with a body double for all I care. It's not like I have any lines, eh? I'm *dead*."

"Dom." Flora lurches to her feet. She leans heavily on her right foot. The left must have fallen asleep. After all, she has been kneeling for well over an hour now. "This isn't you."

"Oh?" Dominic exclaims, throwing up his hands. "We *know* each other now, do we?"

Flora jerks as if he slapped her. "I thought so," she murmurs.

"Yeah, I thought so too," Dominic spits. He slaps at the boom mic hovering above his head, and the operator loses his grip. The pole clatters to the ground, and the sound of audio feedback jettisons through the space. Dominic drags his shirt up over his chest, revealing the same injury I saw earlier.

Except—

It's significantly less red now. The swelling has gone down; the lesions aren't so much lesions as they are red marks upon his skin. The only evidence of pus is a smear of yellow on the inside of his shirt. *Impossible!* It looks as though an entire week has passed in the last hour's time. I can't quite believe my eyes

"I thought this meant—" he starts. But then he presses his lips together, releasing the shirttail bunched in his fist. "It doesn't matter what I thought, does it?" With that, he steps off the soundstage and out onto the lot. The rest of us—myself, the crew, and

Flora—merely blink in the sudden sunlight until the stage door closes on its pneumatic hinges. I should go after Dominic and strong-arm him back on set. Better yet, I should call MGM and tell them that this is the last straw. But instead, I simply stare at the duct tape "x" on stage where he had lain, trying to make sense of what I had just witnessed.

Then, everything slots into place. It was Dominic who hid Flora's face from the camera. Surely, he wouldn't have done that if he was of normal stock. He would have recoiled, run screaming, or projectile vomited upon the ground. Which means he knew what was happening; he knew what she was. Maybe, he's one too. I think back to the books in my office, wracking my brain for any mention of healing factors. Then, yes!

The Wolf-Man can heal at lightning speed. As such, effective euthanasia requires severing the spine, removing the head, or cutting out a necessary organ like the heart or brain.

I can hear Robert Taneca's voice as though he's sitting beside me. *Shoot them first. If you wait, it will be too late. They know what you smell like.* A cold chill sweeps down my spine. I have to act. It seems as though wherever I turn, there are more of them. They are hunting me, inching closer even in the light of day!

"S-s-should we take ten?" Paul asks. He's holding his clipboard against his sternum like a shield, as if expecting me to attack him.

"Yeah, let's take ten."

◆ ◆ ◆

Sunset Pawn is, as the name suggests, just off Sunset Boulevard. While the boulevard is famous for its rows of palm trees, it is an ostensibly seedy place with tourist trap shops selling tchotchkes; panhandlers corralling the ignorant onto buses, promising to show them celebrity homes; and sidewalks littered with pamphlets for faith healers and fortune tellers. The pawn shop is just off the main drag, wedged between a store that seemingly only sells cigarettes and a small cafe that smells faintly of an unclean toilet.

I walk around the block twice before I gain the courage to step inside. It smells musty, and the lingering dust makes me sneeze. "Gesundheit," someone calls from the back of the store. Then, in a softer tone clearly not meant for me, "Gee-*sus*, Eugene, I told you to dust the taxidermy."

Sure enough, when I look at the near wall, there are several animal heads mounted on plaques: a black bear, a deer, and a jackrabbit with antlers affixed to its skull. Beneath it, on a shelf, lounges a leathery-looking juvenile alligator and a handful of mice dressed in miniature frocks. Their sightless and unblinking glass eyes are unsettling, and I resolve not to look at them again. A man—wearing the name badge "EUGENE"—approaches me. He's at least fifteen years my junior, with greasy skin and hair. In a red flannel button-down and too-tight Levi's, he looks like the Marlboro Man, though he lacks the character's suavity. "What can I help you with?" he asks. He doesn't sound like the gravelly smoking cowboy either. Rather, he sounds like he grew up sucking his mama's teat in Orange County. If I wasn't so nervous, I would laugh.

"I'm looking to buy a gun," I manage around the thick lump in my throat. "For home protection."

Eugene doesn't seem particularly rattled by my request. "Sure, pal. Follow me." He slouches toward a small, glass case on the opposite wall. Slapping his hand on the top, he leaves behind a greasy print so clear that I can see the whorls of his fingerprints and the shallow curve of his lifeline. My sister fancied herself a palm reader and would probably say he'll suffer from prostatitis in the future. It was always cock-related ailments with her because it made her clients more likely to buy some tonic she made out of dishwater and jasmine. *You have to be able to upsell,* she'd chuckle, tapping the end of her button nose.

The gun case is lit from within, holding three handguns and a long shotgun resting on ivory pillows. "Any of the handguns would be suitable for home protection." He jabs his index finger at the handgun in the middle. "The Beretta 950 is made for self-defense, and it's so small it'll fit right in your pocket. Plus, it's lightweight: made of aluminum and plastic."

"Would it—" I hesitate, not sure how to phrase the question without sounding like I belong in the loony bin. "Could it take down a wild animal?"

Eugene leans against the gun case, crossing his arms over his chest. "If you're asking if it's lethal, yeah. I mean, it's got a *bullet*, pal. But it might take more rounds to get the job done depending on what you're aiming at."

"What if I was aiming at *a wolf*?" I can't help but whisper the last two words. It feels wrong, like saying "fuck" while sitting in the pews during Mass. Am I really considering aiming a weapon at my actors with the intention of killing them?

Eugene quirks a brow. "Are you planning to go to Siberia or something? You would need a shotgun for that." He gestures at the long-barreled gun. "But if you used this for home defense, you'd blow an intruder's head clean off. It's heavier than the Beretta too, and you can't hide it on your person unless you have a real roomy asshole." He chuckles at his own crass joke.

The shop bell dings. More customers enter—tourists. They have that wide-eyed, slack-mouthed, scream-talking quality that most Angelenos find unpleasant. "I'll just take the Beretta," I say quickly. It's not lost on me that I'm an Academy Award-winning director, and I could be recognized. I pull the bill of my baseball cap over my brow, hoping the shadow will conceal my face.

"Let me ring that up for you," Eugene says smoothly, unlocking the case with a small, silver key. "We only accept cash."

CHAPTER
NINETEEN (DOMINIC)

———◁◆▷———

Ramón Del Olmo barges into my trailer, stomping up the trio of steps with an energy usually afforded to a much younger man. "I don't know what is going on with you," he says, without preamble, "but this little strike of yours has to end. MGM is breathing down my neck." He rips open the curtains, and a swath of sunlight pours into my eyes. I feel like a bat that just burst from its cave after a long nap—disoriented and windmilling in mid-air.

"Tell him that I'm not finishing the movie," I mumble into my pillow. "He can blacklist me if he wants to. I'll move to Cuba." My pillow reeks of stale saliva, but I don't resurface. I'm not in the mood to talk.

"Oh, don't joke about that," Ramón groans. "Joseph McCarthy's spider sense is tingling." I hear the chair scrape away from the dinette table and a little content sigh as he gets comfortable. Plastic crinkles, and I take a peek to find him eating a pastrami on rye half-wrapped in cellophane. He's clearly not going away.

"I brought you a sandwich too," he says, catching my eye, "if you're hungry."

A fount of hot bile jettisons up my esophagus, making me burp. "I'm not hungry," I manage and clap my hand over my mouth. After Flora's rebuff the night before, I did go up intending to go straight to bed, but the bottle of bourbon was insistent that I drink it. I nearly polished it off before falling asleep and finished the remainder in the shower this morning. I managed to stay spectacularly drunk during Flora and I's disastrous scene, but the hangover is creeping in now. God, I wish that had been a real knife, not a prop! I just want to be put out of my misery.

"It's from Langer's Delicatessen, with extra Russian dressing," Ramón wheedles. He brought my favorite. The dense bread and salty meat would soak up the bourbon still sloshing around my belly; it's cured far worse hangovers. But I'm not sure it can ameliorate heartbreak. Still, the smell of the vinegary dressing makes my stomach rumble, and I clamber to my feet. As I slump into the chair opposite my friend, he sagely pushes my sandwich across the tabletop. I pick at the cellophane, and Ramón leans forward on his forearms. "Tell me what's going on," he urges.

"Nothing," I mumble, peeling away the thin plastic and tossing it aside. The sandwich is so laden with meat and cheese that the thin slices of bread holding it together threaten to crumble in my grip. I take a tentative bite, grateful that chewing affords me a few seconds to think of a more acceptable answer. He won't accept the brush-off—he knows me better than that.

"Bullshit. One of the script supervisors told me this morning's scene was brutal to watch."

I can't even remember what I said to Flora. I only knew the words tasted rancid, and I had to scrape them off my tongue. There was no swallowing them down, so I left them curdling in a pile on her lap. A hard lump of masticated sandwich slides down my esophagus in slow motion. "Last night, Flora and I left the party. Together."

Ramón's eyebrow quirks. "Oh?"

"We went for a run, and we were attacked by a mountain lion up on the ridge. She was probably defending her territory or a litter of cubs hidden nearby." Setting aside my lunch, I lift up my shirt to show him the latticework of scratches on my chest. Ramón nearly chokes on his pastrami. A bit of yellow dressing trickles down his chin, dotting his collar. Still staring, he blindly feels around the tabletop for the short stack of napkins but only succeeds in knocking the lot onto the floor.

"Gee whiz," he breathes.

I readjust my shirt. "Flora saved my life, and I asked her to come to bed with me."

"Some 'thank you'," Ramón remarks dryly. "Though, you've never been one to just send a card or a bouquet of flowers." He bends beneath the table to retrieve a napkin and resurfaces with a handful crumpled in his paw. He swipes at his stained collar with the whole fistful but only spreads the mess.

"It wasn't like that." I sigh. "She turned me down."

"Oooo-ooooh," Ramón coos, drawing the word out into an insolent sing-song. He thinks he's tamped me down—gotten at the root of it. "So your masculinity is feeling a little wounded, huh? It's not often anyone says 'no' to Dominic Valentine."

"I *said* it wasn't like that, Ramy," I snap. "I think that I might have genuine feelings for her. I thought, perhaps, she felt the same. There have been little moments between us…" I trail off, embarrassed.

Ramón's face softens, but his tone is still somewhat biting. He isn't done delivering tough love. "Dom, every moment on set has had the two of you sniping. Can you blame her for saying 'no'? Most women don't respond particularly well to being berated. Flora isn't going to fall into your arms simply because you showed her an ounce of kindness."

"It's hard for me," I say, tearing a bit of crust off my sandwich and popping it into my mouth. "You know that."

"Yeah," Ramón sighs. "I know."

"Dom, lend your mama some money," Mildred Valentine *wheedles, holding her cupped palm out the open window of her beat-up sedan. "You know I'll pay you back."*

I raise my eyebrows at her, unable to contain the short guffaw that leaks out from between my lips. I paid for everything she owns, including the Chevrolet station wagon, the string of chipped akoya pearls draped around her neck, the clothes piled in the backseat, most of which still have the Marshall Field price tag affixed to the sleeve or waistband, and the leftovers from Cindy's Eagle Rock. She's only paid me back with misery.

Standing on the narrow sidewalk between bustling Wilshire Boulevard and the more tranquil Hancock Park, I feel as though I'm in a state of flux. I can either hand my mother another wad of cash or I can wave her away. Part of me feels as though I owe her. After all, when I was a teenager, she worked as a teller at the Citizens National Bank in Texas to pay for acting lessons and cleaned houses on the weekends to pay for bus tickets to auditions. Despite her busy schedule, she never missed a curtain call. I could always find her—front row, stage left—clapping and whistling.

But I know she'll spend it getting high with her beatnik friends. What was once her secret vice is now a still-life tableau on her dashboard. She hadn't even bothered to hide the empty bottles of methedrine or the spent cartridges of Benzedrine. The labels have all been torn off.

Her hand, still outstretched, spasms. "Please, Dom," she murmurs, eyes darting, licking at her dry lips with the tip of her pink tongue. "Just a few dollars." At lunch, she barely ate a morsel, busying herself by peeling the golden skin off her fried chicken breast. Despite the chill in the diner, courtesy of the air conditioner directly across from our booth, her high forehead was shiny with sweat. When prodded, she said she was recovering from the flu. But I know better.

She started using methedrine a decade earlier to lose weight and then to treat depression. She often popped a pill before meals or went to the doctor for an injection. She continued when we moved to Los Angeles, but soon, she added heroin to the roster. "I can't sleep otherwise," she'd lamented, "it's as though there are ants beneath my skin."

"I can't give you any more money," I answer. "Can't you see it's killing you, the lot of it?"

"You're killing me," she counters.

Suddenly, from behind me, a flashbulb goes off. "Look! Look! *It's Dominic Valentine!" A group of tourists rush across the grass toward me, holding out autograph books and pens. My mother curses and cranks the wheel, peeling out into traffic.*

"Wait," I call, but she doesn't hear me over the sounds of traffic and screaming fans. A young woman, bouncing on the balls of her feet, waves a red leather autograph book beneath my nose. She can't be more than fourteen, a smattering of pimples on her rosy cheeks.

"Mr. Valentine!" she gushes. "I loved you in Heirs and Enemies! *Can you please sign this?"*

Reluctantly, I take the proffered pen and sign the page next to a squiggle I think might be Jimmy Stewart's signature. Or, more likely, a Jimmy Stewart impersonator dressed in cowboy garb like The Man from Laramie, *stationed outside of Grauman's Chinese Theatre. As I add the final flourish to the "e" in Valentine I try, in vain, to spot my mother's station wagon, but it's nowhere to be seen.*

Mama calls me later from a payphone, her voice crackling over the line. "You're selfish," she cries, without preamble. "You're selfish!"

I sit up in bed, the phone's curlicue cord draped across my chest. "Mama," I murmur, keeping my voice soft and even. I think of the nasty little Shetland pony my grandparents kept on their farm who would pin his ears back and bite if you so much as looked at him cross-eyed. "Why don't we meet tomorrow? I found a treatment center in Malibu for yo—"

It's the wrong thing to say. *"You know,"* she says, her tone biting. *"Los Angeles has changed you, Dominic. Who is this holier-than-thou person you've become? Not my son, that's for sure."*

I sigh. *"Ma—"*

"I don't have a son." She coughs into the receiver. I imagine her leaning heavily against the payphone's cubicle, winded. A pang of regret sweeps through me, as icy cold as an Arctic breeze.

"Mama, you're sick. Let me help. Where are you? I can come get you." I swing my legs over the side of the bed, reaching for the bedside lamp. The warm, golden glow is an affront to my senses after the pitch-dark room, and I squint, searching the floor for my discarded pants.

"I'm doing just fine without you," she chuckles. *"And that's what you want, isn't it?"* With that final barb, she hangs up, leaving me with the keening of the dial tone. The longer I listen, the more the unrelenting tone seems to fluctuate into a plaintive siren. I can't bring myself to replace the receiver in the cradle; it's my only link to her. Once I hang up, she's lost—a needle in a haystack made of two million wefts of straw.

She was wrong; I need her. For my entire childhood, it was just the two of us—a single mother and her snot-nosed kid making do in a one-bedroom apartment in Lubbock, Texas. My father hopped a train to find work elsewhere during the Great Depression and *simply didn't come home. Even when dinner was just a few forkfuls of beans from a Heinz can, we would eat at the kitchen table like proper folk, a votive candle with St. Francis of Assisi burning. "For ambience," she'd say. When I finally got my first proper paycheck—from a guest spot on* The Goldbergs—*she helped me open my very own bank account.*

Finally, I replace the receiver in the cradle, pull on my pants and a shirt, and pad, barefoot, into the living room. Ramón lazes on the couch, idly watching Broadway Open House *on NBC. "This show is garbage," he murmurs. "What I wouldn't give for another channel!" He's been staying with me while his loft is being fumigated, and his insomnia keeps him awake well past the cable network's patriotic sign off. Tonight, I'm happy to find him here.*

"We need to go to Central City East," I announce, searching for my loafers beneath the couch and coffee table. I find one but not the other. I peel off the couch cushion next to the one he's sitting on but only find a squashed pack of cigarettes and crumbs.

"Skid Row?" Ramón wrinkles his nose. "Dom, it's 11:30 at night." I hear what he's not saying just as clearly: it's unsafe.

"I think that's where my mom is. She just called, Ramy, and she sounds horrible. I'm worried about what she'll do." I can't help but picture her in a drainage ditch, her skin sloughing off in the stagnant, dirty water. "She's desperate." And it's my fault, I think. I should have just given her the money.

In the car, Ramón drives slowly down Fifth Street. I lean out the passenger side window, trying to see into the slipshod tents on the sidewalks. Most are occupied, but it's difficult to see by whom. When the headlights strafe over them, the denizens raise their arms to protect their eyes from the bright light or more securely close their tent flaps. On Gladys Street, we find a trio of night owls standing around a barrel with a roaring fire inside. Ramón idles alongside the curb, and I step out.

"Excuse me," I call. "Have any of you seen an older woman: late fifties; long, dark hair; slender build; wearing a string of pearls?" I hope they don't see me as a threat. My hair is unkempt, mussed by my pillow, and I'm wearing two totally different shoes— one brown leather loafer and one black.

One of the men laughs, his hands hovering over the fire. The grooves in his palm are dirty, making them appear cavernously deep. "Pearls? You think some broad with pearls would be on Skid Row? You're pretty far from Beverly Hills, pal."

"She might be using," I reply, digging into my pocket for my wallet. Inside, in a plastic sleeve, is a photo of my mother and me from over a decade ago. I'm sitting on her lap, even though at ten, I thought I was far too old for such things. Her appearance hasn't changed much, though her face is lined with more wrinkles now and her eyes are perpetually drooping. "This is her."

One of the other men hums. "I saw her 'bout an hour ago. I'll tell you which way she was headed for a cigarette if you've got one." He's smaller than his compatriot, wearing an Ushanka cap pulled over his ears.

"Barnaby," the first man chides. "Have you seen the chariot he's riding around in? He's got more to offer than a Pall Mall."

Barnaby sniffs. "I just want a cigarette."

I fish a silver cigarette case out of my breast pocket and toss it to Barnaby. "They're hand-rolled," I tell him. Barnaby opens the case, selects a thin cigarette, and gives it a tentative sniff. Then, he puts it between his lips, leaning over the barrel to ignite the paper. After several puffs, he nods approvingly. "I saw her at the Holy Dove Kitchen. I thought she was a volunteer."

"Where's that?"

"Two streets that way," he replies, jabbing his thumb in a northerly direction. "But it's closed now."

The Holy Dove Kitchen is a nondescript building with a row of card tables lined out on the sidewalk. Various paper signs are still taped to the tables' edges, reminding those waiting for a free meal to "be patient," "keep an eye on your belongings," and "pray every day!" Ramón and I walk up and down opposite sides of the street, peering into the narrow alleys between buildings.

"She's not here," Ramón calls from the opposite sidewalk. "She could be anywhere. Call her house again."

I step into the phone booth just outside of the kitchen, leaving the door ajar. It smells strongly of urine inside the cubicle. Careful not to touch anything, I slot a few coins into it and punch in my mother's phone number with my knuckle. The phone rings, and rings, and rings. When I step out of the booth, dejected, something crunches under my shoe. It's a small, iridescent sphere—a pearl. I pick it up and roll it between my thumb and forefinger.

"She has to be here," I insist, my voice reedy and trembling. I slip the pearl into my breast pocket, and it settles into the rectangular indentation made by my cigarette case. It rests against my chest wall, chilling my skin through the thin fabric of my shirt. I should have worn a coat—it's November and an unseasonably cold day—but it must be adrift in the Bermuda Triangle with my brown leather loafer's mate.

Ramón casts his eyes up and down the deserted street then crosses to join me on the sidewalk. "Should we walk down Fifth Street?" he asks. "Maybe we can get a better look in the tents on foot."

I agree.

Fifth Street's sidewalk is nearly impassable with tents and lean-tos constructed out of cardboard sitting shoulder to shoulder. While there are encampments all over Skid Row, this seems to be the most popular camping spot. I imagine it's because of the streetlights placed every half-block; every nook and cranny is illuminated, which reduces the likelihood of theft or threat. I shuffle sideways to squeeze between a stack of egg crates covered in a blue tarp and a small, olive Armbuster tent with so many holes I assume it was last used on the beach at Normandy.

Then, from behind me, I hear a soft moan and a male voice. "That's it, Millie! Open those pretty eyes. C'mon, baby doll."

Millie! Mildred! *The voices are coming from the drab Army Surplus tent. I wrench the flap back and look into the harried eyes of a man with a rat's nest of wiry, gray hair atop his head. For a long moment, we both just stare at one another, frozen in place. Then, another stifled moan comes from within the sleeping bag he is nearly crouched on top of. "Go away," the man says, baring his yellowing teeth at me.*

"I'll show you teeth if you don't back the fuck up," I growl, pushing him aside. He tumbles as if his bones are as hollow as a bird's.

"Stay away from Millie!" he shrieks, scrambling to his feet. Before he can lunge at me, Ramón grabs him by the arms, hauling him backward. I gently peel the sleeping bag away from the supine figure and brush the long, matted hair off her clammy face. It's my mother, her flesh pale. Since I saw her mere hours ago, she's scratched up the skin of her cheeks, leaving shallow, bloodless gashes that resemble whiskers.

"Mama?" I murmur, patting her cheek. "Mama, can you hear me?" Her mouth falls open, and her tongue undulates as if trying to form words. But all that she musters is a shaky breath. Frantic now, I give her a shake, and her eyes crack open; her pupils are pinpoints.

"She took too much," the man stammers, his arms still pinioned in Ramón's grip. "She just needs to sleep it off."

Her breathing is shallow, and despite her cracked eyelids, I'm not entirely sure she's aware of my presence. "She's dying," I manage, the words tangling in my throat. "Ramy, go to the phone booth—call for help."

Ramón hesitates but releases the man and jogs back the way we came. The man falls to his knees beside me, taking my mother's limp hand between both of his. I want to wrap my hands around his throat and squeeze until the vertebrae pulverize into a fine powder. I want to drive my knuckles into his face until cerebrospinal fluid leaks out of his nostrils. I want to kick him in the ribs until his body ratchets in half.

"Millie's such a nice lady," the man mumbles. "She'll be okay, she'll be okay. She just needs to sleep it off."

Another man, presumably awoken by the commotion, crawls out of a squat hut made of rotting pallets lashed together with nylon cord. He wordlessly clicks on a flashlight, aiming the beam at the tent's back wall. "Leon," *the onlooker says, addressing the man beside me.* "Give her some space, alright?" *Leon acquiesces with a little whimper, shuffling backward on his knees out onto the sidewalk.*

"Her color is bad," *the man says to me.* "See her fingernails?" *He crouches in the space left by Leon, training the light on her slender wrists and hands. Her nail beds are blue.* "She's not getting enough oxygen. Turn her over on her back."

"W-what?"

"We need to push on her back, get some air into her lungs," *the man explains. Without waiting for my assent, he unzips the sleeping bag the remainder of the way and rolls her onto her stomach. He is careful to adjust her dress over her legs, conserving her modesty.*

Then, he gently moves her arms so that they are level with her head, bending them at the elbows. "The Holger-Bielson method," *he explains, driving his palms into her upper back before pulling firmly on*

155

her upper arms. "I may not look the part anymore, but I was a medic in Okinawa."

Two pairs of headlights strafe over the encampment. I crane my neck to see my car, driven by Ramón, and an ivory Packard-Henney combination coach, a pair of red lights identifying it as emergency transport. It bears a striking resemblance to a hearse. A tiny fount of hope erupts within me. She's going to be okay!

She's going to—

The man isn't pounding on her back anymore. He sits on his heels, his pageboy hat bunched in his fists. "I'm so sorry, son," he sniffs as he clambers to his feet. As he passes, he clasps me on the shoulder.

"You can't hold everyone at arm's length," Ramón says gently. "It's not sustainable; surely, you can see that."

"Damned if I do, damned if I don't," I shrug. I pushed my mother away, and she died on the sidewalk. I clung to Penelope Cox, and she flayed me open for all to see.

With Flora, I've been playing a sordid game of tug-of-war. *Which of us will be torn in two?*

CHAPTER TWENTY (FLORA)

———◁◆▷———

"And that's a wrap for Daphne!" Otto announces. The crew claps and whoops, and I grin sheepishly, doing a little curtsy on my mark. It looks silly in slacks, but it seems appropriate nonetheless.

It was a poignant scene to end my tenure on set, Daphne standing in the foyer with her suitcases at her feet, giving the lakeside mansion one last appraisal. It's a silent scene over which a hopeful orchestral score will be played. Daphne is about to start anew, and the audience is meant to be proud of her. Except, as soon as the door shuts behind her, the audience will be privy to something she is not. The music will swell—violins playing a harried glissando with vibrato— as the camera pulls up the staircase. Suddenly, a skulking, fur-covered figure will brush past the lens!

Otto holds out his hand to help me off the stage. His palms are sandpapery, his fingers leathered with callouses. "This feels surreal," I gush. I feel strangely off-kilter. I had expected the end of principal photography to feel like clocking out at the end of a shift. But it feels more akin to leaving mid-shift—lights blazing, door unlocked, and the merchandise unguarded. "I wish I didn't have to wait for the premiere to see it!"

Otto gives me a strange look. Excitement, perhaps? But there's something else too—a quirk of the lip and a darting of the eyes. "I've been working on some of the edits in my office. Would you like to see the scene I'm working on?"

"I would love to," I reply despite the long day and the late hour. My bones feel creaky, and my eyelids are heavy, but this is an opportunity few people ever get. I follow the director up the stairs to the rasping catwalk, gripping the railing with both hands. Climbing into the rafters of the soundstage feels wrong, much like being in an airplane. The telltale prickling of fur sprouting on the back of my neck gives me pause, and I freeze, sucking in deep breaths.

"Are you coming?" Otto asks, already standing outside of his office. He looks impatient, bouncing on the balls of his feet like a child excited to show his mother his art project. I can almost imagine him at six, holding up a piece of construction paper covered in elbow macaroni and globs of opaque glue. Beneath us, the crew disbands, heading home.

"Yes," I answer shakily, taking a step forward. Suddenly, the stiletto heel of my shoe plunges between the diamond-shaped grating on the catwalk, and I stumble. I steel myself for a harsh landing, but instead, Otto's burly arms wrap around my midsection. The director hauls me to my feet then wrenches my shoe out of its trap.

"You have to be careful up here," he says, handing me my shoe. "It's a long way down."

We peer over the railing. The foyer set is at least three stories down, with layers of rigging crisscrossing the empty space where a ceiling should have been. If I were to fall, the rigging would mangle my body, twisting my joints. I shudder.

Otto and I continue along the catwalk. He walks more slowly this time, and I stare at his back to keep from experiencing vertigo. There's a bit of white fuzz on his shirt right between his shoulder blades. I pluck it off without him noticing. "Here we are," Otto announces, veering into his office.

It's a cramped, ostensibly industrial space, barely able to accommodate a desk, a bit of shelving, a stack of cardboard boxes in the corner, and a projector with two film reels mounted on top. The desk is barren, but the strange pattern of dust on the top shows that it was recently occupied by several rectangular objects. Books or stacks of papers, perhaps?

There is only one chair, tucked beneath the desk. Otto gestures for me to sit then fiddles with the projector. He removes the reels and threads in a new one with the care of a father braiding his daughter's hair. "There's a particular scene I actually wanted to show you," he says. "Perhaps you'll have some insight."

"Oh?" I sit, crossing my ankles. Something about his tone makes me feel uneasy. *Did I ruin a scene?*

Otto turns on the lamp for the projector and flips off the room's halogen bulb. The projector hums, and a small square of light illuminates the far wall. It's so small that I have to lean forward, my elbows on the desktop, to get a good view. In the scene, I'm running, a nightgown billowing around my legs. I pump my arms like pistons, craning my neck to see what is following me. Dominic lurches into the shot, dressed as the monster. I catch a brief glimpse of the seam at the back of the suit before the camera angle changes to the two of us in profile. When the Flora on-screen trips, I inwardly wince. *Why would he use this take?*

I look up at Otto questioningly. But his eyes are on the projection. He stands uncomfortably close to my chair, his hand on the backrest. Perplexed, I look back at the scene. I'm on my back now, looking up at the monster lumbering toward me. There's a smudge of dirt just beneath my right eye, dark rivulets beneath following in the wake of my tears. It appears as though my face is cracking open like a porcelain doll's. As Dominic kneels, my lips part, a soft sob leaking through my already cracked veneer. I remember this moment; I'm not acting anymore. This is real—real pain, real fear. "Otto," I murmur, not quite sure what I plan to say. I want him to turn it off. I'm embarrassed.

"Just watch." His hand moves to my shoulder, his calloused thumb digging into the sensitive spot just above my clavicle.

Then, on screen, my face contorts. *Oh!* I try to get up from the chair, but Otto's hand is an anchor. "Everyone told me it was a problem with the film," Otto breathes. "But it isn't, is it?"

"I—" I don't know what to say. I watch as my lower jaw elongates, as clear as day, despite Dominic's best efforts to conceal it with his hands. My tongue noodles out of my mouth, lapping at the air. It looks like I'm a viper unhinging her jaw, preparing to swallow an ostrich egg whole.

"I've been doing research," Otto says, his words coming out fast and loose now. It's as though he's prepared a speech, and he's afraid he'll forget his next line. "About you, and what you are."

"Mr. L-Lang, I don't know what you're talking about." My voice sounds unfamiliar to me as my tongue swells in my mouth. The red wolf is butting up against her cage, gnawing at the bars. I squeeze my eyes shut tight, a single tear dribbling out. *He doesn't know*, I console myself, *he can't possibly know.*

"And," Otto continues undeterred, "I know what I have to do." He reaches around me, his arm brushing against my breasts. I try to lean away, but there's nowhere to go; he's effectively blocked me in between his body and the desk. Slowly, he opens the desk drawer just enough to slip his hand inside. Then, he wrenches it out, revealing a gun, his finger already curled around the trigger.

"Mr. Lang. Otto! I don't know what you think you've seen or what you think I am, but I'm just *Flora*." The words trickle out of my mouth in fits and starts. I'm bargaining for my life, and there's no script for it. "Just put the gun away. We can talk. I'll just sit here, and you can show me what you've found."

"Quiet," he whispers. He rests the hand holding the gun on my shoulder, the muzzle pressed against my neck. The metal is freezing cold—a shock to the system. My teeth chatter.

"I'm not anything," I say, blubbering now. "Just the girl in your movie. Do you hear me? I'm just a girl."

"Quiet!" He jabs the gun against the tissue-thin skin of my neck. "I know about your kind. Wolf-men! Or women, I guess, in this case. *Wolf-women*."

The skin on the back of my hands tingles. I clench the armrests tightly. If I were wearing my fur, I could subdue him. I may even be able to survive a bullet in the scapulae. But the transformation would startle him, and he'd shoot me dead before my vertebrae click into place.

"He told me that you were hunting me, and he was right," Otto babbles. "Why else would you be here? Why else would you have traveled so far, auditioned for *my* movie?"

The cold metal against my neck makes me squirm. All I can think about is what it will feel like if it goes off. Will it hurt—spreading white hot through every nerve ending? Or will my brain even be able to comprehend the pain before the lights go out? *Sorry, nobody's home right now.*

"Stop moving," Otto advises. "You don't want me to miss." He angles the gun slightly so that it is wedged up against my jawbone. "I met a monster like you with a bullet wedged in his spine. He's suspended in time now—wolf and man, living and dying." I don't understand what he's saying; it's as though he's speaking another language, the familiar vowels and consonants in the wrong places.

I am suddenly aware of the rattling of metal. Someone is walking on the catwalk just outside of the office door. I stare at the closed door decorated with a film poster of Lang's *Crazed,* one of the edges curling free of the Scotch tape. Then, there's a triplet of knocks. "Otto?" a familiar voice calls.

Dominic!

"Oh," Otto whispers, his hot breath wetting the shell of my ear. "Should we invite him in?"

I furiously shake my head *no*.

The doorknob turns. Of course, Dominic wouldn't wait for permission! It seems to take ages. When it finally clicks, I manage to find my voice again, squeaking out a strangled "Run!"

But Dominic either doesn't hear me or doesn't understand. He steps entirely into the dark room before he takes stock of the scene in front of him—the projector repeatedly threading through the scene of my accidental transformation, my pale face and shallow breathing, and finally, the gun leaving a kiss mark on my clenched jaw, the color of a bruise.

Dominic's dark eyes meet mine, but he's talking to Otto. "What the hell are you doing?"

Otto straightens, and the gun trails up my cheek. I cringe as it settles at my temple. With a steady hand, he toggles the safety with his thumb. It clicks. "I'm doing her a kindness," Otto replies serenely, "and protecting myself."

Dominic's jaw clenches. "Otto, you sound fucking delusional. That's Flora Wright, the star of your movie."

"Of course, you'd say that," Otto laughs. "You've been protecting her. Hiding her. You know, I have my suspicions about *you* too."

Dominic takes a step toward the desk, and Otto trains the gun on him. Without thinking, I kick off the underside of the desk, tipping the chair backward.

163

The chairback collides with Otto's midsection, and we topple to the floor. The gun goes off, the blast much louder than I expected. It illuminates the room like a lightning bolt, and for a moment, I am aware of Dominic's misshapen face, pain etched into every wrinkle. *Oh god, Otto shot him!*

Otto thrashes beneath me and the chair. Blindly, I slam my elbow into the space I expect his face to be. I make contact, and his nose collapses beneath the hammer strike of my ulna bone. "Ah, bitch!" Otto exclaims, hitting me on the head with the butt of the handgun. Disoriented and blinded by stars, I am as moveable as putty. Otto throws me—and the chair I was sitting on—aside and clambers to his feet.

The carpet is thin and scratchy, the cement beneath sapping all the warmth from my cheek. For a moment, I am certain I have died. But I can't be dead. The pain is a tether, keeping me Earthside.

When my vision clears, I see the underside of the desk and the dust bunnies congregating in the corners. The projector offers a scintillating white glow, illuminating a]tiny cobweb beneath the drawer, a spider busily wrapping a fly in her silk. I can see Dominic too, or, at least, his hands, palms on the floor. As I watch, his fingers clench and his elongating nails rip through the carpet's braided fibers and polypropylene backing. Fur bursts out the backs of his hands and crawls up his quavering forearms.

Slowly, I sit up. My head protests, throbbing painfully. Dark edges fold over my vision, but I blink them away. Otto is still standing where we fell, his hands at his sides. He's forgotten about me entirely, too engrossed by Dominic's contorting body. I am so close I can touch the gun dangling from his fingertips. I lunge at the dazed director and sink my square, human teeth into his wrist. He howls in pain and surprise, dropping the gun. He tries to jump aside, but I don't let go, feeling his tissue-thin skin shear away. Coppery blood pours into my mouth. He raises his hand to hit me, and I let go, cringing away.

Then, Dominic rises, fully formed, on the far side of the desk. In his wolf pelt, he is enormous, his fur somehow darker than the dark room. He stands directly in the projector's beam, my running form cast upon his abdomen. Somehow, the slow-motion setting on the projector had been flipped, and I run at quarter-speed, my fall into the damp grass seeming to take an eon. With a snarl, Dominic grabs Otto by the shirt collar and drags him across the dusty desktop.

With the struggling director in hand, Dominic steps out onto the catwalk. I scramble to my feet, all too aware of his plan. "Dom!" I scream, my voice reverberating through the empty soundstage. "You can't!"

The studio lights are still on—an affront to the senses after the dark office. In the light, I see the blood thickly pouring down Dominic's left shoulder. Otto had indeed shot him, albeit accidentally. But Dominic, as is his custom, doesn't listen to me. As if he's discarding a piece of trash, he tosses Otto off the catwalk.

"No!" I shout, running to the rail. Otto Lang's body ragdolls in the air and hits a light fixture with a hollow *thwunk*. The bulb pops and explodes, showering glass onto the foyer set below. Otto lands on the half-staircase and rolls to the bottom, his neck askew.

I lean against the railing, staring down at the man, willing him to move. He doesn't. "He's dead," I breathe.

CHAPTER TWENTY-ONE
(DOMINIC)

———◁◆▷———

Ramón drops the paper on the table, the flared pages infringing on my untouched plate of pancakes soaked through with syrup. It's the latest edition of *Daily Variety,* a portrait of Otto J. Lang on the cover. The headline is printed in block letters: "Suicide and Scandal! 'Don't Look in the Lake', indeed!"

I scoff, pushing the paper away. In doing so, I inadvertently topple the pepper shaker, and black flakes march across the white tablecloth like a colony of ants. "Are they shelving the movie?" I ask. Ramón sits in the chair opposite mine, scanning the patio for a waitress. He'll order his usual after pretending to hem and haw over the Chateau Marmont menu. *Shakshuka and a side of rye toast, I think. Thanks, love.*

"The opposite," Ramón chuckles. "They mention the premiere date at least five times." He finally manages to flag down a waitress, and I wait for him to complete his song and dance. The waitress knows the game and plays her part. She leans over so that her breasts infringe on the neckline of her blouse. I stare at the image of Otto Lang on the cover until Ramón finally deigns to end the tiresome charade. "Shakshuka and a side of rye toast, I think. Thanks, love!"

With a sigh, I reach for my champagne flute of orange juice. It's pulpy and acidic, and it doesn't sit well in my empty stomach. I can almost feel the fluorescent orange whirlpool in the pit of my stomach, agitating the bile. "What do they say about Lang?" I ask, curiosity getting the better of me.

Ramón leafs through the pages and reads aloud. "'Lang was found dead at the MGM soundstage just after filming wrapped. It's unclear what propelled the Academy Award-winning director to take his life, but Paul Van Houten, Assistant Director of *Don't Look in the Lake!,* indicated that Lang had been withdrawn, missing whole days of filming. 'He was in a bad sort of way,' Paul exclusively told *Daily Variety* over the phone. 'I wish I had pushed harder to get him help.' Lang's latest horror feature may give us some insight into his troubled mind; the themes of loneliness and familial instability ring a little too true to life for the single, reclusive director.'"

"They're practically salivating," I mutter. I stab my pancake, saw off a wedge, and pop it into my mouth. I let it sit too long; it's so soggy it dissolves in my mouth in a truly unsettling way. But everything since that night has been disquieting, hasn't it?

Flora flies down the stairs, her skirt tangling around her legs. A strange keening noise erupts from her mouth, though I'm not sure she's aware of it. I move far more slowly than her, my palm clapped against my shoulder. Shrugging off my fur made the gunshot wound bleed more profusely, and the blood loss makes me discombobulated. Everything has a fuzzy, grey quality, as though I'm midway through a bottle of liquor. I stumble down the stairs, falling more so than walking, catching myself on the rail. I chuckle, slap-happy. Oh, I should get shot more often. I've never felt better!

I make it to the bottom of the stairs on gelatin legs and sit heavily on the penultimate step. Flora kneels in front of me, her hands on my knees. "He's dead," *she says with a moan.* "Dominic, he's dead." *She's very pale, and a trickle of blood edges down her high fore-head from where Otto struck her.*

"Well," *I slur,* "he canna fly, can he?" *I snicker at my own joke, though it sounds hollow, even to me. I didn't want to hurt him. But he was going to kill Flora—and me too. I could see the stalwart resolve in his eyes, clear as day. He thought if he did a terrible thing, it would be for the greater good. I saw the same look in the eyes of soldiers on news reels as they talked about walking into mortar fire. Kill or be killed.*

"What are we going to do?" *she wails.*

The look in her eyes—frightened like a baby rabbit about to be gobbled up—sobers me up. I suck in a deep breath, willing the world to come into sharp relief. My shoulder thrums—a deep ache that courses across my chest and mid-back, squeezing my heart in a vice. "We walk away," *I answer.* "We go back to our trailers, pack our things, and go home. The movie is over. Let it look how it looks."

"How does it look?" She wipes snot from her nose, not bothering to be ladylike about it.

"Like he jumped." I shrug, which causes a lancet of pain to zing through my clavicle like an electrical current. "Listen to me: go back upstairs, get the film reel with your magical morphing face on it, find the bullet and gun, and pick up anything that was knocked over during the tussle. Then, we'll walk out, easy as you please."

Flora nods, skirting past me to do as I ask. Her skirt slaps against my cheek, and I catch a brief scent of her floral perfume and, beneath it, the sulfurous smell of fear-sweat. I listen to the tap-a-tap of her heels on the stairs, leaning my head against the juddering railing. It feels strangely soothing, like listening to static on the television after midnight.

I doze, waking when Flora returns to the bottom of the stairs. She has the film reel tucked under her arm and the gun in hand. The color has returned to her cheeks. "I found the gun but not the bullet."

That means the bullet is still in my shoulder. "Help me up," I urge. Flora grasps my right hand with both of hers then throws her body weight backward to leverage me upright. Stars burst before my eyes.

Together, we walk through the quiet, seemingly abandoned backlot. Most of the cast and crew have gone home, eager to have dinner with their families for the first time in months. I entered the soundstage at dusk, and now, the sun has set entirely. The darkness is inky—almost corporeal. We don't touch, but I can feel her fingers brush against my naked back every few steps. She's ready to catch me if I fall, though the real likelihood is that we'll both tumble to the ground under my weight. Outside of her trailer, she hesitates, her hand on the door latch. "Where's the bullet? What if it's found?"

"I expect I'm about to go dig it out of my shoulder," I reply flippantly. *"See you at the premiere, Flora."*

"Wait." Flora's hand brushes against my arm. "You can't possibly do that alone. Let me help you."

"Are you sure you're up for a party tonight?" Ramón asks, jettisoning me back to the here and now. "You still look ... out of sorts."

He's being kind. I didn't quite recognize myself when I looked in the mirror this morning. *Who's in my room?* I thought, sleep-addled, before realizing I had caught a glimpse of myself while trudging back to bed from the toilet. Since the film wrapped two months ago, I've lost weight. My cheeks are dark hollows, and my eyes are perpetually bloodshot from lack of sleep. The guilt keeps me awake, gnawing at me like ravenous rats. *You didn't have to kill him,* they screech in hundreds of dissonant voices. *You didn't have to.*

Around us, the waitstaff of Chateau Marmont hang lights and arrange autumnal centerpieces on empty tabletops complete with gourds, gold and ivory flowers, and pillar candles. In the adjacent ballroom—with its high, arched, Cathedral-like windows—sit hundreds of carved pumpkins, soon to be lit from within with tea candles. They are a fire hazard and have caused small blazes at previous Halloween galas, but one must make sacrifices for ambience. At last year's event, I fitted a pumpkin onto Ramón's head, and he ran through the ballroom telling anyone who would listen that he was the Headless Horseman. *I can't seem to find my horse, Miss. May I ride you?*

"No," I admit, "but it'll be strange if I'm not here." I've been a fixture at the Chateau's galas for a decade now. If I'm not here, reporters will be sniffing around my front gate come morning.

The waitress returns with Ramón's breakfast. "Can I get you anything else, Mr. Valentine?" she asks, eyeing my waterlogged, drooping pancake stack. I've only managed the one bite. "A coffee? A glass of whisky? We have a bottle of Old Overholt from 1925."

It's only 11:30 a.m., but I choose the whisky. I'll have to be more than a little drunk to get through tonight's festivities.

◆ ◆ ◆

Penelope checks her eyeliner in the mirror outside of the ballroom. She's dressed as Cleopatra, complete with a sleek, black wig and a long, golden gown. I'm Mark Antony, in a linen toga and braided sandals. "Are you going to look dour all night long?" Penny asks, meeting my eyes in the mirror's reflection.

I don't bother answering the question, adjusting the knot of the toga upon my left shoulder. It keeps slipping, threatening to reveal the pink pucker of flesh where a bullet once nestled. I don't want to have to explain it to Penny—or anyone, for that matter.

Penny is still staring at me. "If I knew you were going to be a sourpuss, I wouldn't have agreed to be your date," she grumbles. I shrug. I didn't ask her to be; Ramón did. *Let yourself have fun tonight, pal. You know Penelope is always up for it.*

Penny leads me into the ballroom, dragging me by the arm as though I'm an insolent child having a tantrum. The band is loud and lively, and I recognize the song as a Bill Haley and His Comets single. The room is humid, made balmy by undulating bodies and hundreds of voices speaking at once.

My date leaves my side to say hello to her friends, and I make a beeline to the bar. I order a Moscow Mule, stuffing a few dollar bills in the champagne flute set on the bartop for tips. The bartender is a fast worker, and I'm downing the gingery drink in a matter of seconds. The warmth folds over me like a duvet, and I consider ordering a second. I'm nearly done with the first.

"Dominic?" Flora slips between two partiers and perches on the barstool beside mine. She's dressed as Tarzan's Jane, her brown, two-piece dress revealing a significant amount of toned midsection. Her auburn hair is loose and wild around her shoulders. "I didn't expect to see you here tonight," she admits, fiddling with the hem of her skirt.

"I never miss a party," I reply, pasting on a devilish grin. She gives me an appraising look—clearly not buying the faux enthusiasm. Of course, she doesn't; she was in the trailer that night.

I sit on Flora's couch while she flits around the trailer, gathering materials. She's talking to herself, the words a muddle of half-thoughts I can't quite parse. "This? No, maybe ... oh, yes. These!" Finally, she sits beside me, dropping an armful of towels, a tin with the

*first aid cross emblazoned upon the lid, and a minia-
ture bottle of Cointreau Triple-Sec into her lap.*

"Is that for me?" I ask, eyeing the liquor.

"No, it's to disinfect the wound. Maybe you can
have a nip afterward."

"I'll need more than a nip," I grumble.

Flora places her hand on my naked thigh and gives
it a short squeeze. "Are you ready?" she asks, meeting
my eyes. The gesture is strangely intimate, but haven't
we just committed the most intimate act together? No,
I amend. I did that myself' — she told me to stop.

I nod, taking my palm away from my weeping
shoulder. I crane my neck to see the skin fiery red and
mottled, not dissimilar in appearance to raw, shredded
pork. The entrance wound is small, no larger than the
tip of my index finger. Flora pours some of the Triple
Sec onto the towel. "I'm sorry," she says and pats
the fabric against the wound. The pain is immediate,
bending me in half. Hot tears trickle down my cheeks,
the saltiness coating my lips. "Fuck!" I groan.

"All done," Flora murmurs, rubbing my back in
concentric circles. Her palm is pleasantly cool on my
feverish, sweat-slick skin. When she stops to reach
into the first aid tin, a whine escapes me before I can
swallow it down. The pitiful sound hangs in the air
between us, and I avoid her eyes, embarrassed. Flora
doesn't appear to notice. Or, at least, pretends not
to. "I was a Girl Scout as a kid," she chatters, "but
unfortunately, my First Aid badge didn't cover bullet
removal." With that, she digs into the wound with her
thumb and forefinger, rooting around for the slug. My

vision goes black, and I am only distantly aware of her sweet, sing-song voice. "Almost, almost..."

I wake later, supine on the couch. When I slowly sit up, I find that my sweat has adhered my skin to the vinyl. It feels like I've peeled off a tissue-thin layer of skin. But it's incomparable to the throb in my shoulder; I swear I can feel my heartbeat beneath the square of gauze. The trailer is dark save for the overhead light above the sink.

I need to pee. I am keenly aware of my bladder near to bursting. Slowly, I rise and pad through the narrow trailer. Her trailer's blueprint is identical to mine, albeit slightly smaller. I find the cubicle bathroom easily. After relieving myself, I wash my hands, trying to avoid my reflection in the mirror. I'm not sure I want to see the person staring back at me. Will he look like a stranger? Surely, the act of killing has marked me somehow. Maybe it won't be as evident as the wound on my shoulder, but it'll be visible all the same.

I should go to my own trailer, dress, and head back to my house in Benedict Canyon. But upon leaving the bathroom, I spot Flora laying on the small bed in the rear of her trailer. She's still fully clothed, a bit of my blood streaking the bodice of her dress. She sleeps on her side with her hands clasped beneath her cheek and her knees drawn up to her stomach, crossed at the ankles. As I watch, her brow furrows and her lips pull up at the corners. She's dreaming. "No..." she breathes, a hiccup of a sob following like an interrobang.

"Flora?" I call gently. I'm not entirely sure why I want to wake her. Perhaps it's to free her from the *nightmare. But isn't this a waking one? Which is worse: the monsters in her dreams, or the man whose bones were dashed upon the soundstage? Or perhaps I'm the monster. After all, it was me who threw him off the catwalk, skipping him off the rigging like a smooth stone off water.*

Her eyes flutter open, and she startles, clearly not expecting to see me. "You're awake," she murmurs, rubbing her sleep-crusted eyes with the heels of her hands. Flora's dress is rumpled, as is the hair on the left side of her head. She doesn't bother to tame it. We are past such things. After all, she had her fingers inside of me.

"Were you having a nightmare?" I ask.

Flora blinks at me. "Was I?"

"You were whining in your sleep," I reply, feeling foolish. I should have left without waking her. I should have gone home. Though, the longer I stand here, the less certain I am that I would have made it home. My body is quaking with exhaustion. My knee sockets feel loose and unsupportive; they won't hold me upright much longer. "I-I thought you were—"

With that, my legs crumple. I reach out for some-thing—anything—to slow my descent. I manage to grab fistfuls of the bedsheets, but their silkiness slips through my fingers like water. Oomph. Landing heavily upon my buttocks, a zing of pain travels up my tail-bone. I become aware of two things at once then: my shoulder feels like it is on fire, and Flora's hands are on my face.

"Are you alright?" she asks. She's kneeling beside me now, sitting back on her heels. "You're pale." Her

thumb brushes against my bottom lip. Whether it's by accident or purposeful, I can't quite discern.

It's all too much to bear. I feel torn open, fileted from throat to asshole like a salmon. A sob bursts the levy, and behind it comes a torrent of tears. "I did a terrible thing," I blubber amidst the tumult of my emotions. Flora says nothing. Instead, she lugs me to my feet, tucks me into her bed, and lays beside me. She strokes my hair until the sobbing stops, replaced by bubbly hiccups and whimpers.

I must have fallen asleep because I wake to sunlight and Flora's sleeping face inches from mine. She's sharing the pillow even though it's damp from my tears and sweat. One of her arms is slung around my waist, her nails lightly brushing against my butt cheek. Careful to not wake her, I slide her arm off and lay it on the mattress between us. The bit of jostling makes her face screw up, but her eyelashes don't so much as flutter. I ease out of bed, aching, and leave without saying goodbye.

"Mr. Merlotte made me come," Flora sighs, resting her chin on her palm. "It's 'good for the brand,' he says."

"Oh, is that why you're talking to me? Where are the cameras?" I make a big show of looking out the nearby windows for paparazzi, but of course, there are none. The Chateau takes good care of its guests, and that includes the utmost discretion when they're letting their hair down.

When the bartender approaches, Flora orders a Sidecar. "You know," she says after her drink arrives, tracing the moist rim of her glass with her finger. "I had this drink on the airplane to Los Angeles. My seatmate—an actress—told me this city would chew me up and spit me out. I remember another certain *someone* saying much the same thing."

"Oh?" I take a sip of my Mule, raising both eyebrows in faux surprise. "Why would anyone say that?"

Flora scoffs. "But what I've realized is that you've all been gnawed on. You're all hopelessly insecure— every single one of you. Especially you, Dominic."

It's my turn to scoff now. Flora rotates her stool so that her knee butts up against mine. "When will you ever see me as your equal? Or as a friend? You cling and then push me away like a bad habit. It's exhausting."

Out of the corner of my eye, I catch sight of Penelope dancing with a ginger-haired man I can't be certain *isn't* the comedian Red Skelton. As if she can feel my eyes, she finds me in the crowd, flashing her red-carpet ready smile.

Flora's right.

Even Penelope Cox can be diffident. When we lived together, she would often refuse to leave the house, unable to find a flattering outfit. "I can't wear *that*, I wore it to the Children's Hospital Gala six months ago!" she'd sob, flapping her arms like a flightless bird. "I can't wear *that*—it makes my skin look absolutely *pallid*. Imagine the headline: 'Move Over, Bela Lugosi: There's a New Zombie in Town!'"

I have always clung to Penelope like a buoy, and she relentlessly dumped me into the dark water without ceremony. When she lifted me out—spitting, coughing, and squeezing saltwater out of my hair—I let her stay.

It was better than sleeping with cold feet and colder thoughts. It's become a complicated dance: flirt, fuck, fight, flee, repeat. *Am I doing the same with Flora?*

"I wasn't aware I was *clinging*," I finally say. "That doesn't sound like me at all. Last I checked, I was enjoying a drink *alone*."

Flora sighs. "You're impossible." She gets up from the bar, downs the remainder of her fluorescent orange drink (danger, danger!) and slips into the crowd. She doesn't bother to look back. I've failed whatever test she'd administered.

My nerve synapses jolt, nearly propelling me out of my chair. *Follow her*, my body screams. Instead, I sip my Moscow Mule, letting the warm, gingery vodka go to my head. I order another and hold up two fingers. *Make it a double, barkeep!*

"Whew!" Penelope tumbles into the chair beside me, her cheeks red and sweat glistening upon her chest. "I thought he would never be tired of dancing! It's always 'one more song, one more'! I'm *beat!*" She adjusts her wig, using the polished mahogany bartop as a mirror.

"Maybe he'll hire you as a *Red Skelton Hour* dancer."

"Is my date going to ever ask me to dance?" Penny asks, giving me a sidelong look. "Imagine what people will say if you don't."

I swallow the last dregs of my second Mule. "Sure," I relent, sliding off my stool, though I'd rather do anything else. If I refuse, I'll just sit here mulling over Flora's words, dredging up rotten memories.

The next song is a slow one: Patti Page's "Changing Partners." Penny wraps her slender arms around my neck, her cheek upon my shoulder. Even tucked beneath her synthetic wig, I can smell her hair—sweet like decaying rose petals, the edges curled and crispy. We must look so in sync on the dance floor. After all, we are dressed the part: the Politician and his Queen. But Mark Antony and Cleopatra were doomed from the start, weren't they? Both fell upon knife blades, utterly alone.

I can't stop mulling over Flora's words, picturing her sleeping face awash in sunlight. I can't let her walk away thinking the worst of me. I gently push Penelope away. "I've got to go," I say, breathless. "There's something I need to do."

Penelope's brow furrows. "I don't even get one song?"

"I'm sorry," I add, already striding toward the ballroom's exit. The dance floor is teeming with dancing couples, and I have to weave around them. In the Chateau's lobby, I slap my hands on the check-in desk, startling the woman tending to it. She yelps, dropping her pen. "Can you tell me if Flora Wright is staying here tonight?" I ask, my words a little too loud and fast. I trip over every syllable, the whole lot falling into a pile on the countertop.

The woman's eyes bulge when she recognizes me. "Mr. V-Valentine, we can't give you information on guests staying in the hotel."

"Please, just tell me what floor she's on," I wheedle. "It's important."

Ding! Behind me, the elevator chimes, and the receptionist glances over my shoulder. "Isn't that her?" she asks, gesturing. I spin on my heel, just catching a glimpse of Flora stepping inside the elevator car with a cadre of other partygoers including a man dressed in a fuzzy gorilla costume, the mask tucked under his arm, and a woman with cat whiskers drawn on her cheeks with eyeliner.

The doors are closing. I lunge at them, thrusting my hand inside to force the doors to reopen. "This car is full," Gorilla Man says.

"I'll fit," I insist, wedging myself in. The other passengers grumble at the intrusion but press together to make room. The doors sweep closed behind me, nearly trapping the tail of my toga. I pull the length of fabric tightly around my thighs.

Ding! The doors open on floor three, and several partygoers disembark, chatting excitedly about a mini bar and a jacuzzi tub big enough for five. Now, there's only four people in the car: myself, Gorilla Man, a woman with an updo of cascading barley curls wearing an enormous hoop skirt, and Flora. Flora simply gives me a nod. She thinks this is happenstance; we're just two ships in the night heading to our respective ports.

At floor five, Gorilla Man exits, his rubber simian feet squelching on the marble floor. Queen Victoria—or whomever she's meant to be—follows him, her heels clicking. Just before the doors close, I watch the two furtively embrace, clearly having a clandestine rendezvous.

Flora and I are alone. As the car shudders up to the top floor, I turn to face her. "I'm sorry."

"What did you say?" Flora looks at me with round eyes as though I've spontaneously grown another head. She's never heard me apologize before.

"I'm sorry," I repeat. "You're right; I've been cold and callous. Cruel, even. I don't deserve what I've got, and I don't deserve what I want either." I run my hands through my hair made stiff by pomade. The nervous gesture makes my hands greasy and my hair stand on end.

Flora parts her lips as if to speak, but the elevator interrupts us with a merry *ding*! We're on the seventh floor. The doors slide open, revealing a short hall leading to the terrace penthouse and other, slightly less extravagant, rooms. "I'm sorry," I repeat as if the words are imbued with magic. Perhaps they are because Flora is still standing in front of me.

The elevator doors start to close, but I wave my hand near the sensor, and they open again with a reluctant *clu-unk*. "I don't want you to talk away tonight. Because, if you do, I'll never get another chance," I say in a rush.

"Dominic, what are you saying?"

"You infuriate me. You scratch at my every insecurity. But I needed that, don't you see? I've been sleepwalking for years, expecting everyone to lay on their backs and let me walk over them. I have a lot of people to say sorry too, but I needed you to be the first. Flora, I wasn't delirious that night at my house. I wasn't looking for comfort or a conquest. So tonight, I'm asking you again: come to bed with me."

The motor of the elevator doors hums, a slightly caustic, burning smell filling the car. I need to let the doors close, but I'm not going to—not yet. "I want to wake up beside you again. And this time, I want to still be there when you open your eyes. I regret what I did to Otto. It haunts me. But I'd do it a million more times just to keep you safe," I finish. The air between us feels thick, like the smog pressing down on the city.

Suddenly, she kisses me, standing on tiptoes. Her palms tentatively alight upon my chest, and I wonder if she can feel the fast staccato of my heartbeat beneath the thin cloth of my costume. "Take me to your room," she breathes.

CHAPTER TWENTY-TWO
(FLORA)

———◁◆▷———

Naturally, Dominic Valentine is staying in the penthouse, a semi-private residence on the top floor. In the atrium, with its ten-foot ceilings and crystal chandelier, it is his turn to kiss me. He is much more tender than when he kissed me on set; there's an air of gentleness and chastity that I don't expect. It's as though we are starting over entirely. When we pull apart, I feel suddenly bashful.

Without a word, Dominic leads me deeper into the multi-room suite. The living room is furnished with velvet couches, all of which appear unutilized. I can still see the parallel vacuum lines on the cushions. In truth, I can't quite imagine Dominic sitting here. It's playing at opulence, rather than being opulent itself. I run a finger over the armrest, leaving a squiggly indentation in the velvet.

Through the mullioned windows, I catch a brief glimpse of a private rooftop patio, complete with two alfresco sun loungers and several terracotta planters overstuffed with Ficus plants. A book lays open, face down, on one of the loungers; a breeze ruffles the pages, the sound akin to a bird taking flight. When the cover flaps up, I see a pair of eyes on a blue background: F. Scott Fitzgerald's *The Great Gatsby*. What a strange choice of reading material for someone who is just as rich as Jay Gatsby, and, I expect, just as lonesome!

Beyond the terrace, I can just barely make out the Chateau's garden, the spiky palm fronds inky black against the more purpurean sky. The sliding door had been left partially ajar, and I hear music and chatter wafting up from the ground floor. The party is still in full swing. Distantly, I can even hear the rumble of cars up and down Sunset Boulevard.

A chilly breeze trickles into the living room, and gooseflesh rises upon my bare arms and abdomen. Dominic kisses the skin smooth again. He's being uncharacteristically quiet, shadowing me like a wraith. When I glance at him, I discover that he is stiff jawed, his eyes dark and dangerous. He's holding back, biding his time.

That all changes in the bedroom. As soon as we cross over the threshold, Dominic's mouth crushes mine. His tongue presses past my lips, slithering like a serpent. Sweeping his hands down my shoulders, he pulls down the straps of my costume. The rectangle of fabric falls around my midsection like a girdle, revealing my bare breasts. Exposed to the open air, my flat nipples harden into nubs. "Beautiful," Dominic says with a gasp, dipping his head to kiss my clavicle then the plane of my sternum. His bristly cheek brushes against the curve of my breast.

Dominic falls to his knees before me, kissing my flat stomach. Transfixed, I tangle my fingers in his hair, watching him through half-lidded eyes. He hooks his fingers in the waistband of my skirt and pulls it off my hips. I step out of the puddle of fabric.

Standing before him in only my panties, I feel strangely powerful. On his knees, still fully clothed in his silly toga, he looks like a devoted disciple readying himself to make an offering to some old god. He runs his hands up my legs, kissing the spot just above my sex with dry lips. "I'll try to be gentle," he murmurs. "If that's what you want." His voice is husky, thick with fettered emotion. He nuzzles my sex through the thin cloth of my underwear, making me quaver.

"I won't break," I tell him, all too aware of his hot breath on my skin.

His long index finger slips beneath the gusset of my panties and pulls them aside. Then, he presses his tongue between my sensitive folds, finding the nub that makes me cry out and fist his hair. "Dom," I gasp, jutting my hips forward. Dominic swirls his tongue until I'm panting. My legs shake, and I fear that soon they will crumple beneath me. He cups my ass with his hands, his sharpening nails dimpling the flesh there. *I'll try to be gentle,* he'd said.

Oh, please don't be!

Suddenly, an orgasm ripples through me, and I find myself wantonly grinding my pelvis against his eager mouth. When my body settles, drooping, he rises to his feet and ensnares my mouth with his. I've never tasted myself before—lightly tangy with a hint of sweetness that dissipates on my tongue like merengue. Dominic bites my lower lip, and I hiss; his teeth are keenly sharp now, drawing blood. I feel it trickle down my chin.

It's my turn to undress him now. I push the heavy swathe of fabric off his shoulder, revealing the semi-circular scar just above his armpit. The skin there is shiny and pink. I can't help but think of Otto's bloodless face, his eyes cast heavenward. "Does it still hurt?" I ask.

"No," Dominic assures me.

The toga, free of its mooring, pools at his feet. He kicks it aside, still wearing the ugly sandals. It's startling to see him nearly naked, clothed in only a tight pair of y-fronts. His chest is broad and mostly hairless, and his dusky pink nipples tighten when I kiss them. I rest my hands on his tapered waist, toying with the waistband of his underwear. He growls, the sound reverberating through his chest. "Don't tease me," he grumbles. "I can't stand it."

His cock is already hard, tenting his underwear. I slip my hand beneath the waistband and encircle him with my hand. His cock is girthy and vascular, the turgid head dribbling precum. When he thrusts into my hand, my palm quickly becomes slick with it. I release him, and he makes an unhappy sound deep in his throat.

I kneel before him, the carpet rough upon my bare knees, and carefully pull his y-fronts down his muscular thighs. His cock bobs as it emerges from its enclosure, and I open my mouth for him. "God," he breathes as he slides into my mouth. At first, he is content to let me suck and lick, exploring every ridge with my tongue. But then, he gathers up a fistful of my hair, thrusting hard into my mouth. The head of his cock butts against my hard palate, delving so deeply my nose brushes against his pelvis.

After several impossibly deep thrusts, he urges me to my feet. We tumble together onto his bed as if we are of one mind. It's unmade, and I smell him on the rumpled sheets. Dominic's body is heavy on mine as he sucks the thin skin of my neck between his teeth. I imagine the brand he's left there—a jagged quarter-moon, the mirror image of the scar on his shoulder.

When he props himself up on his palms, his eyes are glowing orbs; they reflect the meager light of the moon outside, the twinkle lights on the terrace. He adjusts himself between my legs so he can slide into me, gasping when our hips jut together. I mewl, raking my fingernails down his back. The pain is kindling to our fire, and our bodies move in unison, stoking the flame into a veritable bonfire.

Suddenly, Dominic cums, his butt clenching beneath my palms. He lets out a strangled howl, rolling off me to lay upon his side. After his breathing slows, he slips his hand between my legs. He's not done yet.

When I wake up, I am cognizant of two things: I'm alone in bed, and I can smell breakfast. The mouth-watering scent of maple and grease draws me from between the sheets, and I quickly pull on my panties to pad into the living room.

The sliding glass door is wide open, and the chill makes my nipples pucker. I pull a waffle-knit throw blanket off one of the ugly velvet couches and wrap it around my shoulders. There's a room service cart in the room, piled high with decadent offerings of pastries including muffins chock full of ripe blueberries, platters of sausage and eggs, a short stack of buttermilk pancakes, two tiny pots of maple syrup and honey, and a carafe of coffee. I surreptitiously dip my finger into the maple syrup then pop it into my mouth. It's still warm.

"I wasn't sure what you liked," Dominic says, leaning against the sliding glass door. I squeak, my cheeks reddening in embarrassment. It feels as though I've been caught with my hand in the cookie jar. Dominic is dressed in a pair of pressed slacks and a polo shirt, his hair still damp from the shower. I can just see the hint of a bruise above his collar left by my lips. "I can order more," he adds.

"I can eat any of this?" I ask, my mouth watering. I feel positively giddy at the prospect. Carver Merlotte would have a conniption if he caught me eating carbohydrates. Sugar would stop his heart entirely.

"Of course."

I tuck the blanket beneath my armpits and pile a bit of each offering onto a plate. Then, I follow Dominic out onto the terrace. He's clearly been awake for some time; there's an empty plate, save for a smear of syrup, on a small glass table, a coffee-stained mug alongside it. The paperback I spotted the night before is now closed, facedown.

"It's beautiful out here," I remark, looking out at the Chateau's grounds. It's still quite early, and the dewy grass refracts the morning sunlight, giving everything a glimmering quality. It's as though the ground has been littered with diamonds. I imagine the rich party-goers drunkenly stumbling out onto the lawn, dropping precious stones from their pockets like loose change.

"It's one of my favorite views in the entire city," Dominic replies. "It might be the front runner after that oversized *cat* put a damper on the canyon."

I perch on one of the loungers, balancing my plate on my knees. The pancake is so fluffy that I can cut it with only the edge of my fork. I pop it into my mouth, delighting in the sugary, yet floral, taste of vanilla. An overstuffed sausage link with its peppery overtones is the perfect chaser. Dominic is uncharacteristically quiet while I eat, his eyes on the gray expanse of West Hollywood on the horizon. He looks pensive.

"Do you ever wish you'd never come here?" he finally asks. "To Los Angeles, I mean."

I'm not entirely sure how to answer that. Since arriving, I've felt like a stranger in a strange land. Los Angeles looks much like anywhere else, but it's as though it's being perceived through a mirror. Nothing is quite what it seems. No one says precisely what they mean. Everyone has secrets, most of them dark. But I've found passion here, in my career and outside of it. "No. I'm glad I came."

"Sometimes, I wish I hadn't," Dominic admits. "This fucking city took so much from me."

I would chuckle if it weren't for his morose tone. Dominic Valentine could have the keys to the city if he'd like. He is a household name, often mentioned with the same longing sigh as James Dean and Rock Hudson. His house is so enormous that it can be described as labyrinthine, and his garage is stuffed with luxury automobiles. Los Angeles has elevated him, placing him upon a golden pedestal.

Dominic pulls his wallet from his slacks and shows me a photo in a trifold holder. The plastic is semi-opaque, giving the photo a murky quality. It's as though the woman pictured is underwater. It's an old photograph which had clearly been handled frequently before it was slipped into the holder. The edges are soft, and a water stain blooms across the subject's face, making her look jaundiced. The woman in the photo is sitting on a low rock wall, her face upturned toward the sky. The sunlight threads through her hair, making her appear as though she's glowing from within. "This is my mother. Her name was Mildred. Millie."

Was?

"She was a Texan, through and through. Prideful. I didn't see what was happening until it was too late. It was like I was blind to it because it was outside of my spotlight. It took until she broke down crying in my kitchen, begging me for cash, before I noticed the track marks on her arms. A few months later, she died on the sidewalk in Skid Row." When his voice wobbles with emotion, he swallows it down, his Adam's apple bobbing.

I set my half-finished plate aside and move to sit beside him on his lounger. When I touch his arm, he collapses like a sandcastle at the beach. He snuggles close, his cheek upon my chest. I smooth his hair, which smells faintly of the Chateau's sandalwood and jasmine shampoo. "I'm so sorry," I say, knowing that the words sound altogether meaningless when pasted against such an enormous loss. It's akin to putting a bandaid on an infected dog bite, isn't it?

"I never told anyone about her. Ramón was the only one who knew her because he practically lived at my house when we were children. When she died, we said that she was his aunt so that no one knew she was related to Dominic fucking Valentine," he mumbles into my cleavage. His breath is hot on my skin. "Her funeral was just Ramón and me watching the grave-diggers fill the hole."

"That sounds like a lonely way to grieve," I murmur. I find myself thinking of Nico's burial and the shiny black casket being lowered into the dirt. We'd topped it with a bouquet of pimpernels and roses in various hues because we weren't sure which color he would have liked best. Even when you know someone for years, sometimes you forget to ask even the most basic of questions. *What's your favorite color? If you died, would you want to be buried or burned?* At the grave-side, I found myself feeling unmoored, as though I would topple in at any moment. But then, as if they could sense it, Mags squeezed my hand, and Ama wrapped her arm around my shoulders.

"I can't believe I let this industry turn me into this jaded person," Dominic says, sitting up. His eyes are wet. "Someone who thinks my mother is expend-able—just debris to be swept under the rug and out of sight. I have destroyed every relationship I've ever had because I've treated them the same way. But I want to try to be better. With you."

EPILOGUE
(DOMINIC)

————◁◆▷————

D espite the tinted windows, I can still see the flashbulbs on the red carpet. It looks like an electrical
storm, and I find myself leaning away from the car
door, remembering my mother's childhood warning.
Don't touch metal, she'd say, *unless you want your
hair to stand on end!* Then, she'd tickle me, making
electrical noises. *Bzzzt!*

"You're next," Ramón announces. He's in the front
passenger seat, his foot on the dashboard, watching the
cavalcade slowly putter down Hollywood Boulevard.
Despite the driver's exasperated sighs becoming more
and more theatrical with every passing block, he hasn't
moved his foot. It's the studio's car, so what does
Ramón care if it's a little scuffed?

I adjust my cufflinks and tie, checking my hair in
the rearview mirror. It's perfect—not a single hair out
of place. I wonder how much I could pay the driver
to speed past Grauman's Chinese Theatre. I imagine
the press dropping their cameras, slack-jawed, as the

shiny sedan veers sharply onto North La Brea Avenue. Perhaps we could go to the In-N-Out drive-thru instead and eat food with our fingers.

"She's here," Ramón says, interrupting my fantasy. "She just got out of the car in front of us."

I lean between the driver and passenger seats, trying to catch a glimpse, but the crowd has already swallowed her up. I hear them shouting for her, trying to get her undivided attention long enough to snap a front-page-worthy photo.

My driver eases the car forward, lining the back door up with the red carpet. "Showtime," Ramón says before climbing out first. He takes his time, always the consummate showman. After all, nothing builds an audience's interest as much as suspense. I snicker as he glances at his reflection in the side mirror, adjusting the lapels of his tuxedo, before finally reaching for my door handle.

As soon as the door is cracked, the flashbulbs start. Even after hundreds of premieres and events, I am effectively blinded, emerging from the car by touch alone. I raise a hand to wave at the crowd, plastering on the widest smile I can muster. "Dominic, Dominic!" the crowd screams as one entity. Before I can even take a step, the questions start:

"Who are you wearing?"

"Have you seen Paul Van Houten's cut of the movie? Does it live up to Otto Lang's vision?"

"Are there wedding bells in the future for you and Flora Wright?"

"What do you think of Penelope Cox's new beau?"

I let Ramón lob answers back into the crowd ("Balmain. Not yet. No comment. We are delighted to hear of Penelope's recent engagement and wish her the best"). I'm distracted, trying to catch sight of Flora.

I find her just inside the theatre being fussed over by Ingrid. Her publicist looks more than a little frazzled. Her platinum hair is a puff atop her head, making her look like a startled feline. "You could have given the reporter from *Confidential* a little something," she frets. "They're curious, and curiosity sells."

"We decided not to say anything," Flora reminds her, her tone more than a little exasperated. She looks radiant tonight, wearing a crimson tulle and lace gown with a high neckline. It gives her an aristocratic air, which is punctuated by the Art Deco diamond necklace adorning her throat. She catches my eye as I approach and offers me an impish half-smile. I kiss her cheek, not wanting to smear her lipstick.

Our relationship is no secret. A photographer caught her leaving the Chateau the afternoon after the Halloween gala wearing one of my suit jackets over her Jane Porter costume. They published the photo alongside one of me wearing the same jacket that morning at breakfast with Ramón. I imagine the person who put two and two together felt particularly proud of themselves.

"What are we going to do?" Flora asks, jabbing a finger against her photo. "I'm sorry. I should have taken it off. But it was chilly in that stupid costume." She is windswept and red-cheeked from the outdoors, and when I take her in my arms, I find her skin is icy.

It's not often that California has a cold snap, and she's certainly not dressed for it, wearing a pair of trousers and a cropped blouse.

"They think we've been together for months," I remind her gently. "We have nothing to hide—not any-more." Flora looks unconvinced, and I don't blame her. Dominic Valentine and the print media go together like oil and water. But when I told her I wouldn't sweep her under the proverbial rug, I meant it.

"But—" Flora counters, but I shush her, kissing her hairline. I slip my hands beneath the hem of her blouse, finding her breasts clad in a silk brassiere. The fabric is slippery and thin, and I urge her nipples into peaks with my thumbs.

"I will go onto the roof and scream until they hear me, Flora. I love you." With that, I pull her down onto my white leather couch, my mouth colliding with hers. The paper clenched in her fist falls to the carpet.

But we've kept some news close to the chest. We want to savor it, like the last bit of melted ice cream at the bottom of the cone. That's always the sweetest bite.

"You have to announce it soon, while there's still buzz," Ingrid wheedles.

"Let Paul have his premiere," I say, referring to *Don't Look in the Lake's* assistant director. He's on the other side of the lobby with some of the MGM executives and looks more than a little green around the gills. After all, he had big—and talented—shoes to fill. "We have plenty of time."

The lights flicker. The movie is about to start. I offer Flora my arm, and we walk into the theatre. We are seated near the front. When the room grows dark and the credits begin to trickle across the screen, Flora leans into me, resting her cheek on my shoulder. I don't watch the movie but instead, close my eyes, listening to our voices as we deliver our opening lines. It feels like such a long time ago now, but I still remember them by heart:

"George, this big old house—surely it's too much for us," Daphne says.

"Perhaps," George replies. "But haven't you pictured it? Imagine how this house will sound filled with children—our children!"

"Dominic," Flora whispers, giving me a nudge. I've fallen asleep. For a moment, I feel discombobulated. *Where am I?* "You're snoring," she hisses.

The movie is at the halfway point. On screen, Daphne runs from the monster that was once her husband and doesn't fall. Instead, she leaps from the dock into the water. The darkness swallows her up, and the audience gasps. "Let's get out of here," I urge Flora, my voice low.

"We can't *possibly*," she protests with a gasp.

"We'll be back before anyone notices," I fib.

Together, we quietly leave the theatre. No one seems to notice, too engrossed in Otto Lang's nightmarish vision of marriage and madness. I lead Flora out of a back door, knowing that we will be mobbed if we go out the front.

"What are we doing?" Flora asks, still whispering even though we are utterly alone.

The alley is narrow and stinks of garbage. It's dark, the only light just above the door we exited out of.

"We're going for a run," I announce, taking off my tie and tossing it into the dumpster.

Flora laughs. "You're off the cob! We can't run through Los Angeles."

"We're only a few blocks from Runyon Canyon," I say, tossing my suit jacket into the dumpster too. I unbutton my shirt.

"This dress is borrowed. So is the necklace."

"We'll come back for them later." I unbutton my slacks and pull them down. Flora giggles at the sight of my pale legs.

"It's a *dumpster*; everything will stink," she argues, but she's less convinced now. Her resolve is wavering.

"I'll get it dry cleaned." Clad in just my y-fronts, I must look ludicrous standing in the middle of the alley. I grin. "Besides, isn't it important for a pregnant woman to get her exercise?" At the mention of the baby, Flora's palm alights upon her still-flat stomach.

Flora presses her lips against mine then turns so I can access the zipper on her dress. "Fine, *fine*! Hurry up, before anyone sees."

END.

ACKNOWLEDGMENTS

I want to thank my family for buying me a word processor when I was in middle school; Carleigh, for everything and then some; Tatum West, for teaching me everything I know; Reddhott Covers, for this gorgeous cover; and the powerful, magical women at 4 Horsemen for believing in me and this story.

ABOUT THE AUTHOR
BEAU LAKE

————◁◆▷————

B eau Lake is a tattooed, blue-haired, queer romance writer skulking around the mountains of Virginia. She is very happily married and lives with a menagerie of children (2), dogs (3), and plants.

Her current hobbies include digital art, social/animal activism, and screaming into the void. Mostly the latter. She is passionate about ending greyhound racing in the United States and worldwide, and shares her home with a retired racer named River. Other favorite activities include listening to true crime podcasts, staring at empty Word documents while having existential crises, and asking herself "What Would Stephen King Do?"

Beau writes both traditional and horror/supernatural LGBTQIA romance. Werewolves are her favorite because they have sharp teeth and even sharper personalities.

Some of her published work includes the well-received DC Pride series, co-written with Tatum West

(Proud, Out, and The Space Between Us). The Wolves of Wharton is her first supernatural series, with more to come!

She can be found online via Facebook, Twitter, or at authorbeaulake.com. She loves t3alking with readers and can be reached at authorbeaulake@gmail.com. Vegetarian recipes are also appreciated.

facebook.com/beau.lake.77

facebook.com/groups/1813967932089935
Twitter @beau__lakebeaulakebooks.com

OTHER BOOKS

Co-authored w/ Tatum West:
Proud, Out, The Space Between Us

BY BEAU LAKE:

The Beast Beside Me
The Beast Within Me

4 Horsemen Publications

Romance

Ann Shepphird
The War Council

Emily Bunney
All or Nothing
All the Way
All Night Long
All She Needs
Having it All
All at Once
All Together
All for Her

Lynn Chantale
The Baker's Touch
Blind Secrets

Mimi Francis
Private Lives
Second Chances
Run Away Home
The Professor

Fantasy & Paranormal Romance

Beau Lake
The Beast Beside Me
The Beast Within Me
The Beast After Me
The Beast Like Me
An Eye for Emeralds
Swimming in Sapphires
Pining for Pearls

D. Lambert
To Walk into the Sands
Rydan
Northlander
Esparan
King
Traitor
His Last Name